The Theory of Happiness

Brody Lane Gregg

ALL RIGHTS RESERVED

Publisher's Note:

This is a work of fiction. All names, characters, places, and events are the work of the author's imagination.

Any resemblance to real persons, places, or events is coincidental.

Solstice Publishing - www.solsticepublishing.com

The Theory of Happiness

By

Brody Lane Gregg

To Jessica…I love you to the moon and back.

Part 1

All That Is Left

Chapter One
The Afterlife

"In one way or another, happiness is the goal of all people. Whether or not they will all reach it, is the question."

~Edward McClage

The metal of the cylinder is pressed so hard against my forehead that I just know the mark is imminent—a large circular bullseye, if you can imagine. Well, that's if it doesn't blow my forehead completely off. I would imagine in that case that there would be at least a gaping hole—a stream of blood. I push harder against the barrel. The gun is hard and cold, but I like it.

"Are you happy now?" he asks, the gun steady in his hand. I hear the poet McClage's words in my head. "Happiness is the goal of all people."

Laughter ensues. I push even harder. "Never happier. Go ahead and shoot me!"

The gun fires. I die, knowing that I lied, because happiness will never be a part of my life.

And that's how I imagine my demise.

***

Screw happiness. It's an elusive feeling, the bastard child of pain and regret. That child that only goes home on the holidays but lives the rest of his or her life practicing a never-ending disappearing act. Seriously, who has time to be happy when there are so many other horrible feelings to occupy one's mind? I certainly don't.

In fact, this emotion—happiness—is as useless as sobriety. There's really no point. Much like the *happy* memories I'm told I should cherish, I find a sober day a waste.

So, I'm confident in saying today will *not* be a waste.

I'm either drunk or stoned. Probably both. It's hard to tell since I've been in this state for the last six months. I've always had an addictive personality, and it's easier to stay this way than to deal with the massive hangovers that accompany a lapse of excess.

My home paints the picture of my frivolity. Empty beer bottles and pizza boxes are strewn throughout the living room. A shattered bong in the corner. And there, in the middle of the floor, lies Pete, vomit caked on his face. Even the darkest of souls needs friends—and drug dealers. Pete is great at his job, that is, if he's not joining in on the party. I don't really remember inviting him over, but quite frankly, I don't remember much of anything that happened this weekend. Or last week. Or the last month. Did I mention I have an addictive personality?

"Thanks," a woman says, struggling down the stairs. She pushes hard against the railing, the old wooden spindles rocking back and forth. Other than her uneven gait, she is a pretty woman. Long blond hair, slender frame, scantily dressed. As she walks out the front door, I wonder how much money she got out of me. If I knew where my wallet was, I'd find out. For all I know, she has my wallet.

I laugh at myself, though really nothing in this situation is funny. I laugh a lot when I'm not sober, or so I've been told. I can't remember.

All of my days start the same, supreme disappointment followed by the extreme desire to self-medicate. Questions like *"How can I get more alcohol?"* and *"Where's Pete?"* are the norm. Unfortunately, Pete's on my floor. That means I'll have to go out. I've been living like a vampire for months now, so the thought of the sunlight hitting my eyes makes my already-pounding headache throb even worse, if that's possible. But I have no choice. The full throngs of the hangover will come soon enough.

I force myself up off the couch and sidestep the garbage. My head pounds, my body aches, misery lingers. I have to summon the energy from who knows where just to make the first step. This is the *me* when I'm not self-medicating. This is the *me* that is forever sick, depressed, and would rather die than stay this way.

Slowly walking up the stairs, beautiful eyes stare back at me from fancy frames. I don't look at them. They are only reminders. As I pass by them, I curse God for the miserable state that I am in. Why do I torture myself with this? I'm not exactly sure, but I've never had the guts to take the pictures down.

The bathroom is directly across the upstairs landing. The walls are green—her favorite color. I can't change them. Another reminder.

Our toothbrushes sit on the ledge above the sink. Mine is red, hers is green. I use hers. Brushing my teeth, I stare into the cracked mirror. Dark circles dot my eyes like an exclamation point reminding me of last night's bad behavior. Protruding cheek bones, pale skin. I am not the man I was six months ago, how could I be? I smile to see the dimples on my cheeks. Those are still the same. That was her favorite part of my face.

Splinters snake their way up the glass as my fist slams into it. *So stupid.* Now my knuckles are bleeding—everywhere. But it doesn't really matter. I'm so numb to the pain anyways—the physical pain at least. It's the mental pain that matters, the anguish. That's what I need to cover up.

I take a cold shower and imagine what it would be like to be washed away like the water that disappears down the drain. I don't bother to shave. I'm not trying to impress anyone. I just don't want to look like a homeless man. Not that there is anything wrong with being homeless. Most of my friends—the ones I get high with—are homeless. But there's always that chance that if I go outside, I'll see someone I know from my former life.

It doesn't really matter that I've showered. None of my clothes are clean. I pick up some dirty jeans off the spare bedroom floor. I don't use what was once *our* bedroom. I can't. Her scent is still on the pillows, in the sheets. I'd rather die than lay on that bed, breathing in the scent of her perfume, my mind telling me that she is lying next to me, only to wake up with the realization that she is not. Slipping my shirt over my freshly washed hair, I take a moment to look in at the familiar sight—rumpled yellow sheets with a crisp white duvet. The bed is still a mess, the way she left it. Some of her clothes: two sweaters, four t-shirts, and a pair of jeans are stacked on her dresser, not to mention a pair of her shoes on the ironing board by the window. It's like I've memorialized the room. Her silver necklace still sits on the nightstand by her side of the bed. And the letter. That forsaken letter. Still unopened…

A few seconds is all I can bare, then I'm walking back down the stairs, staring straight ahead, cursing the row of pictures again. I stop short of halfway down.

"And stay out!" I hear a familiar voice yell.

Pete is being shoved out the front door, a feminine hand firmly on his shoulder. I immediately contemplate running back up the stairs and hiding. Or jumping out the window. Too late.

"I see you!" she yells.

I let out a disgusted sigh. "What do you want Eliza?"

She doesn't answer. Instead, I hear a mix of groans, unintelligible mumbles. And I imagine a number of eye rolls. "Get down here!" she yells after a moment.

The window would have been a better option. Slowly, I saunter down the staircase, shoulders dropped, head down, like a child who has just been disciplined. Eliza is scanning the mess of my home. She looks at me wildly while picking up a newspaper from the dirty coffee table. The headline reads: *Gerhard: A Colossal Collapse.* She shakes her head and throws the newspaper into the filth. "Do you see what you're living in?" With one hand, she grabs an empty beer can, the other, she points toward the dining room, which is just off the main living area, not a clean place to stand around the large farm table.

"What, no good morning coffee and bagel before you accost me?" I grab the door handle. "Just get out."

She throws the aforementioned beer can on the floor, before gingerly walking through the filth, attempting to keep her white dress and matching handbag from touching anything. Eliza, my hard-headed sister-in-law, former cheerleader, prom queen, and twice Miss Tippecanoe County runner up, now turned storefront owner. Eliza, the biggest roadblock to my current lifestyle.

"*Wesley Gerhard*, this is disgusting," she says, shaking something from her black high heel shoe.

I point to the door, urging her to keep walking. "You should be used to this. Your store is filled with this crap."

"The antiques in my store make money. This…" she again points toward the disaster. "… is a waste of money. A waste of a life."

"My life."

Eliza places her palm on the door. "I've left too many times these last few months. I'm not leaving today."

Even through my migraine, through the constant haze of depression, I force a smile. Eliza, the blonde-haired bombshell, spoiled rotten princess, is used to getting her way. In my former life, I might have listened. Not today. "You're leaving. This is my house."

She stands firm. And for a moment, we have a staring contest. For all of her antics, she can be intimidating if she wants to be.

"What do you want me to do?" I finally ask. "I'll clean this up later. I promise."

"Don't give me that crap. We've been through this before. Look at this place. All the collectibles, the furniture she bought to fill your home, all of it, is just a collection of moldy food and beer cans. How do you think sh—"

I place my hand over Eliza's mouth. "Don't you dare speak for her! She's dead, Eliza. Dead. You cannot speak for her now. No one can. Now, if you want to stay here and play housemaid and pick all of this up, be my guest. But I'm going out."

I remove my hand and open the door. Eliza doesn't stop me. Lucky me. Then I see a large figure waiting on the front porch. My brother. By the smirk on Eliza's face, this was planned. They expected I would bolt.

"This is only getting better," I say, as my brother, Roman, walks inside.

"Hey, Wes, it's good to see you," he says in his typically soft-spoken manner.

In case you were wondering, my name is Wesley, Wes to most everyone else except my mother. And *my wife*... but she's gone.

Roman is my twin, three minutes older. He looks like me, but is taller, more muscular. He has the same dark hair, the same blue eyes, the same dimples. If not for his size, and the hair on his face, we could pass as identical.

He embraces me tightly, his overly bulky frame smothering. He was a three-time body-building champ in the local junior events and was pegged as the strongest man in our high school. He's perfect for Eliza. Power couple back then. Business couple now.

I force myself out of his grasp just in time to see the disgust on his face.

"This is way worse than the last time we were here," he says, surveying the destruction.

I see tears forming in his eyes. As big as he is, he's the softest person I know. Especially when it comes to me. It's a twin thing I guess. "I just can't believe this," he adds, wiping the tears from his swelling eyes.

The beep of my answering machine goes off, followed by the robot-sounding operator. *One old message. Seventy-two new.* Eliza stands beside the small table on the other side of my couch, hovering over the phone. She reaches for the red button.

The pit deepens in my stomach, and I immediately run, moving garbage out of the way. Too late. Jessica's voice comes across the speaker. She says my name just before I can press the pause button on the answering machine. The sound sends shock waves through me. Pain. Guilt. Sorrow.

Eliza looks horrified. She places her hand on my shoulder. "I'm sorry. I didn't know you still had a message from her."

My own set of fresh tears burn to be released. That voice—her voice—is the most beautiful thing I've ever heard, but seeing Eliza's tears, well it opens the scars in a way so painful, I cannot cope. Her voice is as beautiful and as all-encompassing as a lunar eclipse, but like an eclipse it brings darkness.

Eliza slides her hand away and smiles. "Now, let's see what new messages you have. I know Jessica's parents have been trying to get a hold of you. And you know your own parents have tried. In fact, your father called this morning, wondering if we had seen you lately."

"Well, now you have," I say, before sitting on the couch, burying my wet face in my hands.

Roman sits down beside me, placing his arm around my shoulders. "Mom and Dad just want to know you're okay. And so do we. And so do her parents. You were as much a part of her family as you are ours."

"I can't talk to them. I can't see them. I only see her in their faces."

Neither of them respond. Instead, the machine beeps as Eliza begins to go through my new messages. Most of them are from my parents, very sad, somber messages just wondering how I'm doing, if they can come and see me, or asking me to just give them a call. A few of them are from her parents, telling me that I'm still a part of their family, and even if she is gone, they still want me to come around. That they love me like a son.

I can't stop the tears from coming full force.

Other messages were from other family and friends offering their condolences and, some of them, telling me wonderful things about her that I already knew.

"Stop!"

"Just one more." Eliza tilts her head.

There's no point in arguing with her. "Whatever."

Message twenty-two. *Hello, Wes, this is Joseph over at the art studio. I know it's been rough these last few months, and I know you haven't taken on any new projects lately, but we have a unique opportunity down here. We'd like you to come chat with us about it. We're meeting to discuss the project on June thirteenth at nine in the morning. We'd love for you to be the one at the helm on this one. Well, I guess if we see you, we see you. But please consider it. You know, we really loved... I mean... I can't believe she's gone. Okay... well... goodbye. June thirteenth at nine.*

It was just like Joseph to say goodbye and then repeat the date and time again.

"That's in a few days!" Eliza squeals like a twelve-year-old girl. "You should do it, Wes."

I can't help but laugh at her stupidity. She just doesn't understand that all I want to do is get high and drink myself to death.

"What's so funny?" Eliza asks.

"Your ignorance." I reach for a cigarette.

"So, I'll take that as a 'no'?" Eliza says, a devilish expression on her face.

I nod.

"Why not?" she asks, deflated. "You're not doing anything. And we can't keep paying your bills. We can't keep giving you money, so you can pay for drugs and alcohol and cheap sex. What would Jessica have said about this—this side of you?"

Hearing her name again shoots pain through my chest. I put my hands over my ears. "Don't say her name!" I yell. "Just get out. I don't do that anymore. It's all gone. All of it, and I don't want to see any of it ever again. I'm done with art. Done!"

"But you both dedicated your life's work to—"

"There is no *we* anymore," I say. "She's dead, remember? Can't anyone just remember that? There's only me and I'm not doing it. I don't care about that. I don't care about anything. What is there to care about? She's gone."

I turn to Roman and see tears streaming down his face. *Stupid softy.* He grabs for his wallet and starts pulling out twenty-dollar bills.

"What are you doing?"

"Helping you change your life," he whimpers.

I put my hand over his. "I don't need your money. I've never needed it. Stop trying to help me."

Eliza huffs. "Yeah, well, how you gonna pay Pete and buy more hookers if we don't pay for it?"

I have every intention of calling Eliza every debasing name I can think of, but Roman places a stack of twenties in my hand. He forces my fingers around the money. "I have a proposition."

"If it gets Barbie out of my house I'm listening."

Eliza glares at me.

"This is five hundred dollars," Roman says. "It's yours to go buy all the drugs and alcohol you can get your hands on, as long as you promise me you'll go and talk to Joseph at the studio on the thirteenth."

I can make five hundred dollars go a long way. As much as I don't want to make any deals with my nosy family, my hangover needs to be numbed. I'm starving for a drag, thirsty for some Jack.

Roman looks at me expectantly. "Well?"

I shake my head. "And I don't even have to take the job?"

"Of course, you—" Eliza starts.

"No, just go to the meeting," Roman interrupts.

"Roman!"

I smile at Eliza. "Deal. Now get out of my house, Paris."

She points at me. "Who are you? For the record, it's not Barbie or Paris, or skank or whore, or whatever else you want to call me. And you better make it to that meeting or else."

Or else what? There's nothing she can do that could hurt me. I've already got that under control. But there's no use telling her that. Instead, I agree and ask her to kindly leave and go kill herself.

Like every other time Eliza has left my house in the last few months, she walks out the door pissed off and complaining.

Chapter Two
Steps

"I'm just not feeling well," Jessica says.

"Then go to the doctor."

She smiles, that smile that tells me I'm doing something wrong. I'm being short with her. I'm not helping. I'm hurting.

"I'm sorry," I reply, but it's not genuine.

"Me too." She opens the door and leaves. I barely acknowledge her absence. She'll be home. That's one thing I can always count on. She always comes back home.

***

The city of Lafayette sits in Tippecanoe County, a historically relevant place if you actually care about American history. Other than that, its proximity to Purdue University, and the fact that it lies directly between Chicago and Indianapolis, are the only things Lafayette can tout on its resume.

And then there's the art studio. Downtown Main Street. A gem in the rough row of shops, law offices, and antique stores. World renowned according to the papers. Sometimes, my picture would be in the papers too. But that was then. That was before she was gone.

I walk down Fourteenth Street, a very cold morning for June, enjoying the wind as it bites at my skin. It's nice to feel something other than my headache for a change.

I'm neither drunk nor stoned today. Just hungover. A two-day binge has left me sick and weak, but half alive—alive enough to brave the chill and keep my promise. Although, I really have no other choice. My money is gone.

This trip would have taken two minutes if I still had my license, but I lost it two months ago when Pete and I slammed into a pole across town, totaling my car. That's what happens when you leave an open bottle of Jack on the floorboard, along with several spent beer cans. Pete had two joints stashed away in his coat pocket. He got away, I didn't. I spent two days in a jail cell until Roman came and rescued me while also paying my stiff fines. In the end, I lost two nights of excess, what little dignity I had left, and my ability to drive.

When I reach downtown, it's lifeless, the expected state of a Wednesday morning. I briskly walk past the line of shops and practically run past the small antique store on the corner. 'Gerhard's Collectibles' the sign says. I laugh through my throbbing headache. The sign should say 'Gerhard's Crap and Other Junk.' Though I pass the storefront quickly, I can still briefly see Eliza's thin frame through the main window. I hope she doesn't see me.

It's only two doors down. The Art Studio. Yes, that is the actual name. It wouldn't have been my choice, but no one ever asked me. Five minutes until opening time, so I sit on a small black bench beside the door, breathing into my exposed hands for warmth. I could use a drink right now, some fire for my throat, but the lint in my pockets can't buy a thing.

"You actually came," I hear a familiar voice say some seconds later. It's Joseph. The old, thin man sticks his keys into the door. "We hoped you would, but we just weren't sure."

I turn toward him, and by the look on his face, I know he sees a pale ghost of the man that once worked here. "Let's just say I had no other choice."

Joseph smiles beneath his beard. "There's always a choice, Wes." He looks down at his watch. "Our meeting isn't until nine. You're a little early."

I stand. "I know. Don't worry about me, I'll entertain myself."

Joseph holds the door open. "Well then, after you."

The smells of paint, chalk, and cheap wallpaper hit me first. A sweet scent, one that I've grown familiar with, but haven't had the pleasure of indulging for some time. It's warm and quiet and dark inside, but the latter is taken care of seconds later. Once Joseph has the lights on, I take in the long hall of paintings, hundreds of them.

"It's been a long time," Joseph says, stepping up beside me. He grabs my coat and begins to pull it off. I let him.

I take a deep breath, pulling in the scent again.

"The meeting will be in the conference room." Joseph adds, while hanging our coats and his hat on the small rack just inside the glass door.

I nod, then start down the hall. There are no Van Gogh, Picasso, or Da Vinci prints in this studio. The Art Studio is a place for local artists—painters, sculptors, woodworkers—and scrap artists like myself. Though the greats do not line these walls that doesn't mean that they aren't professional. Nothing goes on these walls if it isn't purely magnificent, a masterpiece, worthy of world recognition.

I was once world-renowned. For my nearly fifteen minutes. Now, I'm barely hanging on to the edge of the earth, almost fading into oblivion, reaching out for Death's gentle touch. These thoughts remind me that I need a hit, or at least a drink. I'm shaking now. Withdrawals tug at me like a passionate lover. Typically, I give in to her. Today, I cannot.

The end of the hall opens up to the rest of the studio, but before that, there are several small offices. One of them still has my name on it. *Wesley Gerhard.*

The door opens easily, blasting me with the thick, musty air of an office that has not been opened in some time. In the doorway is a messy stack of mail, I'm sure letters and job offers alike. Joseph was kind enough to slip them under the door, not disturbing my workspace at all. Even through my headache, I feel a relief wash over me.

This was my true home. My artwork is strewn throughout the closet-sized space. Metal pieces of junk welded together in odd shapes and designs.

My claim to fame—pieces of junk pieced together to the imaginations of my mind. It's stupid really. Why anyone would want to buy this crap…it's ridiculous. For a moment, I feel bad for ragging on Eliza and Roman's antique business. In this brief moment of clarity, it seems hypocritical. The feeling fades quickly.

On my desk is the piece I left half-done that day when Joseph broke the news. Those terrible words. I shake the memory away before it can take me. Now, that piece sits, waiting for the hands of a craftsman to finish it—hands that do not exist now. I place my palm over the cold metal, rusty barbed wire from a farm outside of Lafayette, snaked around an old fragment of a support bar from a recycled park slide.

This piece is me. Its life stopped one day. The same day. Yet, this piece withstands the time. It does not destroy itself. It may take years, even decades, but this metal will decay, rust, fall apart; I will do the same in much less time. Look what six months has already done to me.

I am less than this; I am less than a half-finished, decaying piece of metal artwork.

For the next hour, I stare at it. I stare at myself.

"It's time," Joseph says, his head peeking around the door.

I wake to reality, nothing more, nothing less. Only an even stronger headache tells me I'm still alive.

Joseph is quickly gone, and I'm left staring at the doorway.

And I see her. The first time we met.

My heart aches worse than my head. I feel sick. I feel angry. I feel alone.

***

"Hi, can you help me with something?" she asks, just after knocking on the doorframe.

I look up from a piece I had been working on for months, probably covered in grease and dirt, probably looking like a lunatic. "It depends on what you need."

She steps into my office, extending her arm from her thin frame. She's beautiful. Long, blonde hair, pale skin that seems to shine under the light. "My name is Jessica. I'm here for the receptionist job."

I regret shaking her hand, transferring whatever grime I have on my palm. I pull my hand away quickly before dumbly rubbing my dirty fingers through my hair. "Sorry. My name is—"

"Wesley Gerhard," she interrupts, before timidly giggling. "You're pretty famous around the area," she adds, trying secretively to wipe away the filth from her hand onto the back of her dress pants.

***

I was so embarrassed, so enthralled, so in-love-at-first-sight, that I couldn't say another word to her. Instead, I led her to meet Joseph, awkwardly avoiding any other conversation. She had no qualifications for the job Joseph had told me later. I begged for him to hire her. He was hesitant, but he did. And that was the beginning of the end.

The conference room is directly beyond the main art gallery. I pass several of my pieces, newspaper articles, magazines, press releases taped to the walls behind them. I can remember working on each and every junk pile. Hours of my life. Wasted hours.

When I reach the conference room door, I take a deep breath before entering. I just want to get this over with. Keep my promise to Roman and leave.

Joseph greets me first. He acts as if he didn't just see me moments ago. I shake his hand and he offers me a seat. I refuse.

And then there's Bob. Grumpy old Bob. The two of them are a team, have been for over twenty years. Joseph runs the show, Bob pays the bills.

"It's good to see you," Bob says, his double chin rolling with each word. He sits on the opposite end of the conference room table. "We've missed you around here, Wes."

"You've missed the money I bring in," I respond.

Joseph chuckles, Bob raises one eyebrow. "We certainly didn't miss your attitude," he says. He leans his plump, suited body over the table. "We miss her a lot more though."

I have nothing to say to that. Everyone would say the same thing.

"Why don't you just take a seat and pretend like you care about this job we have for you."

I grin at Joseph's perceptiveness. I don't care about this job at all. That's one thing we can agree on. But I comply and sit down.

"Can we get you something to drink?" Bob asks.

I see the bottle of bourbon in front him. Bob always has a drink in hand. "I'll take what you're having."

Joseph stands up and walks over to a small tray of liquor bottles and glasses. He grabs the bourbon and opens it up.

"Just bring me the bottle," I tell him, just before he starts to pour it. He looks to Bob, who nods in approval.

I polish off what is left in the bottle—maybe a glass or two—as soon as he hands it to me, then I slam the thick glass down on the table.

Bob smiles, baring his ugly teeth. "I heard you were quite the self-destructive one as of late."

Joseph just stares at me, his aged eyes are filled to the brim with concern, glossy even. I'd seen Joseph cry before. The day he delivered the news. I'd never seen something so pitiful. I'd give up all the alcohol and drugs in the world to never see it again.

I slide the bottle toward him. "Don't get all sentimental on me. I'm here to talk about a job, not about my current situation."

Joseph seems to choke back whatever emotions were there a moment ago. He clears his throat. "Right."

"Hold on." Bob raises his fat hand. "Looks like we have the rest of our team." He waves. "Come on in, sweetie."

The door opens, and a young woman walks in. Ebony skin, shaved head, tall, and lean. She looks like she belongs on a runway, not in a conference room with a drug addict, a rich slob, and a sentimental curator.

"Thanks for having me," she says. "But my name is Montica, not sweetie."

Bob shakes her hand, no worse for the wear. *Chauvinist pig.* Joseph courteously stands up and takes her hand next. "We're glad to have you Montica. Please, let me introduce you to—"

"Wesley Gerhard. The famed artist who fell off the face of the earth," she says, interrupting him.

I reach out my hand. "More like jumped off," I respond. "Still falling in fact."

She smiles, perfect white teeth against her dark skin. "Montica Barrough. Nice to finally meet you," she says, shaking my hand firmly

Bob claps. "Well, now that we're through the introductions, let's talk business. Montica is here with a special proposition, one that will bring in money and promotion for the gallery."

"A proposition that will also help my clients," she adds.

She's feisty, a complimentary figure for Bob, who tends to walk over people with his words and actions. She reminds me of, well, me.

"That's what he meant," Joseph follows, always pulling Bob out of the holes he's dug for himself. I'm convinced that if Bob didn't pay the bills, Joseph would have dropped him off on the corner of hell years ago, then watched him burn for a while. Of course, Joseph would never admit to that. He's too proud and proper for that. "You see, Montica is a Senior art major at Purdue University, and she's also a direct support specialist at the A. W. A. Resource Center in central Lafayette."

"The A.W. what?"

Montica takes a seat beside me. "A. W. A. stands for adults with abilities. We're a center that specializes in training adults with developmental disabilities to become productive citizens in their perspective communities, focusing on the abilities that they do have."

She lost me at A. W. A. "What does this have to do with me?"

"Everything," Bob blabbers. "The A. W. A. Resource Center has commissioned us to do an art piece for them in commemoration of one of their beloved clients who died last year. It's a one hundred-thousand-dollar job, Wes."

I can see the rigidity in Montica's body. She exhales, then turns toward me. "His name was Roger, and he was a force in the community. He was loved by all and never allowed his intellectual disability to get in his way. He was an inspiration, and we want to remember that. The community wants to remember that."

"He was retarded," Bob says.

"Bob!" Joseph gasps, disgusted.

"What?" Bob says, shrugging his shoulders. "I'm just trying to help explain the situation."

Montica has a fire in her eyes. She looks as if she is going to hurl over the table and strangle the fat pig. Instead, she turns toward me. "I'm going to try and forget your insensitive boss's rude behavior and just cut to the point. We want you to work on this project. A sculpture that covers the entire façade of the building. Something that will catch the eyes of the public, something that will lead them to read the dedication we have planned for Roger."

It sounds like a noble cause. But I'm not interested. I'd told Eliza that I was done with art, and I'd meant it.

"So, what do you say?" she asks.

Joseph is leaning over the table. If there is anyone who has ever wanted me to succeed more than my brother and sister-in-law, it's him.

But I have to disappoint. My heart just isn't there anymore. It never will be. I lost that part of me six months ago, and I'm afraid it will never come back. "I'm sorry, but you're asking the wrong man. I'm done with art. For good."

Joseph looks utterly downcast. Bob has a smirk on his face, as if he'd known what my answer would be the whole time.

The beautiful young woman allows another smile to form on her lips. "I understand. We thought you'd say as much, but we wanted to try. I can't say I'm not a little disappointed. I've always wanted to work with you. I've followed your work for years, and I must say I'm pretty thrilled just to be here with—"

I hush her with my hand. Flattery is not going to work. I stand up from the table. "I'm sorry, but nothing you can say, no amount of flattery, and no amount of tears…" I say the last part while looking at Joseph, "… will get me to do this." I nod. "Thanks for the offer, but I think it's time for me to leave."

I grab the door handle and open the door.

"How about fifty thousand dollars to the artist?" Bob says.

I stop.

"He's right. We're offering to split the payment fifty/fifty. Fifty thousand dollars to the gallery, and fifty thousand dollars to you. You're worth it."

I squeeze the door handle until my hand hurts. Every part of me wants to run out the door, but all I can think about is the amount of drugs and booze that I can buy with that kind of money. Payment like that is unheard of. No artist would pass it up.

"And we're willing to pay half up front," Montica continues.

An even sweeter deal.

"And all expenses—lunches, supplies, miscellaneous—will also be paid for," Joseph adds.

Now, I can't help but laugh. They've got me by the throat and I can't get away. Money. The one thing I need most in order to get what I want. And they're offering me a year's worth of good salary to put up some pieces of junk on a wall.

I hate myself for succumbing to a decision that I'd promised myself I would not make. I'm here to make my family happy. That's it.

Letting go of the door handle, I release the pent-up aggression inside of me in one long exhalation. They've won. I turn around and look at this super fan of mine. "And I suppose you will be the one helping me, both for your job at the center and for a grade for school?"

Montica grins. "You would suppose right."

"Does that mean you're in?" Bob asks.

I give my best disgusted expression before answering. "I don't really have a choice."

Joseph is beaming. "What did I tell you earlier? You always have a choice."

He's wrong. The fact that I'm standing here whoring myself out for drugs and alcohol proves that I don't.

After shaking all of their hands, I ask the only pertinent question. "So, where's that first twenty-five thousand?"

Chapter Three
One Night in London

"Tears of loss may not drown out our hope in Heaven. The bitter things of life point only above."

~Edward McClage

Edward McClage was a joke. His words are like the filth that washes away from my dirty body, drowned out by ice cold water and drained into the waste of humankind. He knew nothing of real life. Sure, he's been dead for some eighty or so years, but it's his type of optimism that is hard to destroy. It reeks of deceptiveness, and I'm sure if he were alive today, he'd preach his poison to the ravenous appetites of the mass ignorant.

But she loved him. I have no idea why, but Jessica could not get enough of his meaningless crap. All of his books are still stacked on her nightstand—untouched. Every freaking one of them. I don't know how many times she quoted his asinine poems, but it was a lot. The fact that I remember them so well makes me hate the guy even more. He had a quip for everything—and I despise him for it.

But it's his words on loss that really piss me off. I wonder if the guy ever lost a loved one in his entire life. In my morbid thoughts, I picture him dancing at the grave of his wife and singing at the graves of his children. I bet he was a sick individual at heart. He had to be.

I have other methods for the 'bitter things' of life. Unfortunately, no amount of ice cold water can make the pain of loss go away. And quite frankly, no amount of booze or drugs can either, but at least they have some numbing properties.

Now, it's the physical pain that wracks my body. Withdrawals. I haven't had any drugs or alcohol in over a day. Now that I have a job, Roman's pockets have run dry. And I don't get the first half of the money until the day I start the project, which is still a few days away.

Needless to say, I'm dying.

A slow death, only made more painful by an invitation to have dinner with my family. I think I'd rather die than sit around a table and eat with them, but it's my only chance to beg Roman for more money. I know, I'm pathetic.

For the first time in months, I walk into what was once *our* bedroom. I need to get dress clothes from the closet. My brother and sister-in-law live a more extravagant lifestyle, and if I'm going to ask for money, I need to at least act like I'm trying.

I don't know if it's the flood of memories or the withdrawals, but I shiver as I walk by the bed. I can almost feel her warmth against me, our bodies tangled together against the sheets. I can also almost see her beautiful face, resting on the pillow beside me, the morning sunlight casting a glow on her skin, making her look like an angel. What am I saying? She was an angel.

I'm struggling to choke back the tears by the time I leave the room. I swallow hard and force the pain back into the deep vault, hidden away like the words from that last letter. The one still on her nightstand, unopened. I need drugs to do the work for me. I remind myself that's why I'm doing this tonight. For money. For drugs. For the numbing effect that keeps me going.

Fifteen minutes later and I'm walking past the pictures above the staircase, ignoring her beautiful eyes staring back at me. And then I'm out the door.

It's a ten-minute walk to my brother's mansion. It's in the historic neighborhood, not five blocks from my own. As I walk down the broken sidewalk, the mix of large and small *normal* houses turn into large historic mammoths. Mansions that I would have once been able to afford when I was the famous one in town. But Jessica never let us spend our money on a bigger place. There were always more *important* things, like giving to charity or to the church.

I laugh at the thought. I went to church once. What good did that do me? God must really hate me. Well, if He didn't then, He does now.

I take a deep breath as I step up to the brick goliath. It's a gaudy place with white pillars and arched windows. It has Eliza written all over it. I'm halfway content walking around the neighborhood for a little while longer, but I see Roman's face peering out the window. The door opens seconds later, and my hulking brother waves me in. His muscles bulge through his green polo. With his yellow shorts he reminds me of a steroid-filled pineapple with legs. I can't help but laugh as I walk through the door.

"What's so funny?" he asks.

I shake my head. "Oh, nothing."

If the outside of the house is spectacular than the inside is on a different plane. The entrance opens up into a large open room with a balcony and a sitting area just underneath. All decked out in antique accents with a mix of modern furniture. It's beautiful and artistic from an artist's standpoint. But I won't tell them that.

On the other side of the sitting area is an island with a massive marble-laden kitchen behind it. I see Eliza working behind the counter, another woman next to her.

"She's a friend from church," Roman says, placing a hand on my shoulder.

I give him my best frown. "Don't tell me you're trying to—"

Roman smiles, shifting a few steps behind me, in case I turn and run. "I promise, it's not a blind date. She's newer to town. Just got a job here five or so months ago. And we invited her over. We just happened to invite you as well before your new gig."

I don't believe him. I know Roman's lying face, and he's giving it to me. He corrals me into the dining area. I don't fight it, but make it clear with my body language that I'm not happy about the arrangement.

"Just go with it," Roman says, his hand clenched on my tight shoulders. "I know why you're here," he whispers. "I know you want money. But we can talk about that later. Only if you oblige and allow Eliza to entertain. Only an hour or two."

"One hour," I quickly say, before sitting on the sofa. Roman nods.

"Perfect timing," I hear Eliza say, her voice way too bubbly. I feel a headache coming already, which is weird because I already have one from the withdrawals. "Come on in to the dining room and we can eat."

Roman continues to smile as if his fake happiness will somehow float through the air like a contagion and take over my body. I bite my lip in return and follow Eliza into the dining room.

The table is set up like a Thanksgiving dinner—fine china, neatly folded napkins, and an extravagant meal.

There are six places set. I continue to bite my lip and don't ask. *One hour* I remind myself. I take a seat at the far end of the table. "This looks good," I politely say.

Eliza is beaming, wearing an elegant black gown with a white belt. As usual, her hair is done and her makeup unblemished. "Thank you, Wes." She places the large ham in the center of the table. "But I can't take all the credit for this."

Before she even finishes the sentence, the other woman steps into the dining room. She looks to be around

Eliza's age and has that older-woman type of beauty about her. Long black hair and dark green eyes. She, too, is dressed neatly with a sundress and sheer red scarf. She places rolls beside the ham.

Eliza steps back. "Wes, this is my friend, Tessa. Tessa, this is Roman's brother, Wesley."

Tessa extends her hand and I shake it. Her hand is smooth and warm.

"A pleasure," she says timidly.

"So, how old are you?" I ask.

Roman coughs. Eliza looks horrified.

Tessa pulls back her hand and looks at me like I just asked her to kiss me or something.

I shrug my shoulders. "What? I'm just trying to figure out why you would be trying to set me up with an old lady."

The room fills with gasps. "Wesley!" Eliza shouts. "How rude!"

"It's fine, I'm thirty," Tessa calmly says, before taking a seat. "And this isn't a set-up," she continues. "They would never set me up with a drug addict, woe-is-me, used-to-be-famous child."

Roman coughs to hide his laughter. Even Eliza snickers, though her eyes still reflect shock.

I give my first genuine smile. "Good, because I'm twenty-six and that would just be weird." I respect her wit and honesty. And it's only four years difference, but I'm just being mean.

Eliza glares at me as she takes a seat. From the head of the table, Roman, who is still trying to stifle his laughter, mouths *one hour*.

"Well, let's eat," I respond.

Roman, in his ever-pompous Christian-religious-something way, prays over the meal, and then we begin to eat. It's quiet for a moment as we all dig into the wide array of food. Eliza finally tries to clear the air of awkwardness by asking if Tessa is enjoying her new job.

"Very much so," Tessa replies. She turns to me. "I hear you have work coming too?"

With a mouthful of potatoes, I nod, chew for a second, and then swallow. "Yeah, got to get my drugs so I can continue my used-to-be-famous, woe-is-me child's drug addiction."

She smirks.

Eliza clears her throat.

I'm practically full in five minutes, so I broach the subject of the other two settings. "Can you tell me who else is coming?"

Eliza and Roman both stop eating, and I can tell neither wants to answer. They look at each other before Roman takes a deep breath and responds. "Mom and Dad really want to see you. They're on their way now."

It takes everything in me not to trash the table. A one-hour dinner with the promise of a cash advance was just too good to be true. My family of liars. One would think that after six months of being ignored, my parents would get the hint that I don't want to deal with their sorrow, their nurturing kindness, and pretty much everything else that they bring along with them. Of course, leave it to Roman and Eliza to set this up. They meddle just as much as my parents do.

I choke down all the angry words I want to say and fill my mouth with water. By my estimation, I only have forty minutes to go.

Eliza smiles at me. "We wanted them to come and celebrate some news we have. We've already told them, but we wanted to share this with you too."

Roman stands up and puts his arms around his wife. One of his hands moves to her stomach.

"We're expecting," Eliza says.

This time I can't choke back my feelings. Naturally, they would bring me here to rub their happy lives in my face. To kick me when I'm down. To do anything to make my life a living hell. I feel the pit in my stomach, and flashbacks of memories flood my mind. I feel pain, much worse than what my withdrawal headache could ever produce.

I feel my fist hit the table. Tessa jumps at the sound. Eliza falls into Roman's arms. I stand and point at her. "This is all about you. Like always. I'm here for your freakin' money, and that's it. I don't care about your perfect life and fake feelings. I can't do this. I can't pretend that everything is okay and celebrate with you. I just can't."

I see flashes of Jessica in my head, her standing in the bathroom, looking longingly at me. The tears in her eyes. The same tears I saw the day she died. The day she walked out the front door. The day she was taken away from me.

"I have to go."

I practically run out of the house. Slamming the door behind me, I run for the road, straight through the neighbor's perfectly green lawn.

"Wesley!" I hear a familiar voice yell after me. But I don't turn around. I can't look at my dad's face. I can't see him or Mom. I can't deal with them. I just can't. So, I keep running.

I round the corner of 9th street before I finally stop. My breathing is shallow, but I continue to walk away. I have to get as far away from them as I can. Far enough that they won't try to find me.

"Well, that was really something." She sounds winded. "You're fast. I just barely caught the direction you went."

I pause. Why is she following me? "I'm not into older women," I say between deep breaths.

Tessa steps up beside me. "Get over yourself." She grabs my arm. My first instinct is to pull away, but her grip is tight. She pulls me along.

"What are you doing?"

"Taking a walk with a new friend."

I try to pull away again, but don't feel the need to yank off her arm. "No, why are you following me? Just let me go."

Tessa stops, then holds out her other hand. There's a folded up one-hundred-dollar bill in her palm. "I just want to talk. And besides, I won't give you your brother's money if you don't oblige." She smirks, then continues to pull me along, though not so forcefully now.

I need a hit. I need that money. But I'm not going to steal it from her. "Whatever. But why do you want to talk to me?"

She laughs. "Because you're not the only screwed up person in this world you know. I've been where you are. Several times. Is there somewhere close we can sit down?"

"Columbian Park is a ten-minute walk," I answer. My mind follows the logical path and I realize now why Roman and Eliza invited us both to dinner. Not to set us up, but to help me. If she's had a rough life, then maybe she is their last hope.

"Well, I'm game if you are," she says, still pulling me along.

I sigh, then force myself away from her grasp and grab her hand, before pulling her across the street. "Let's just get there and make this quick."

"Whatever you say."

Neither of us say another word until we reach the park. Ten minutes of silence and brisk walking. Ten minutes of me staring at her other hand, the money calling out my name. Her hand is limp in mine, but I don't let go. That's the fear in me talking, that she might leave with the money if I don't drag her along.

Columbian Park is nothing special, summer water park and zoo aside. Jessica loved coming here. I remember when I used to hold her hand as we'd walk around, people watching and talking evenings away.

Memories like these are crippling.

Tessa pulls away from me, and finds the nearest swing. Like a child, she falls into the swing and sways back and forth with the wind. "You can join me if you'd like."

I choke back bile as I see Jessica sitting in that same swing. Her smile. I shake the image away and saunter to the swing beside her.

"You have tears in your eyes," Tessa says softly.

I wipe them away and force my eyes to a tree not twenty yards away.

"I know all about you," she continues. "About your fame, the death of your wife, your downward spiral. It's a sad story."

"One that doesn't seem to end," I respond coldly. "And everyone knows about me. I'm a local news headline. Next stop, obituary."

She laughs.

I turn to her. "What? What could possibly be funny about that?"

She coughs her smile away. "I just remember thinking those things before. Several years ago."

"And what did you lose?"

"Everything," she says, her dark eyes becoming empty. "Everything," she repeats, her own set of fresh tears appearing.

I stand up. I don't have time for her sob story. "Just give me the money." I reach out my hand. "My life is bad enough as it is. I don't need to hear about your crappy life too."

Tessa wipes the tears away and smiles. "Then I won't talk about it. Let's change the subject."

Let's not. "Come on," I whine. "Let's just forget about all of this and call it a day." I need to get my night started. My head is throbbing and the desire for a drink or a hit is overwhelming.

"Alright," Tessa cheerily says. "But first, tell me one thing you want to do in your future. Just one."

"Die." That's an easy question to answer.

Tessa laughs again. "Then why haven't you killed yourself yet?"

"I… uh…" There's really no way to answer that question. Why haven't I done it yet? I've thought about it a million times. Every time I pass the picture frames on the stairwell, every time I see our bedroom, the letter, I just want to die. I just want to be with th—Jessica again, if that's even possible. But none of that answers her question.

"I don't know."

Tessa stands. "It's because you still have things to accomplish. You still have things you want to do."

I shake my head. "No, I don't." There is nothing I want except to get numb, followed by a long blackout.

She grabs my hand. I feel the money on my palm. I clutch it before she can take it back.

"I promise you, there is more that you want to do, or you would have just killed yourself a long time ago. I've been there before. I know what you are feeling." Tessa wraps her arms around me.

My chest feels like it is about to explode. The last time I was embraced like this by a woman—that I wasn't paying—was just after Jessica's death. My mother squeezed so tight I could barely breathe. I haven't seen her since. It was a close call tonight.

I wiggle my way out of her grasp and take two steps back. In the setting sun, I can't help but see this woman's beauty. Older or not, she is striking. But she is not Jessica. She does not have long blond hair, blue eyes, and glowing skin.

"I have to go."

Tessa nods. "I know."

I turn and start to walk away, but a nagging question enters my mind. I want to keep walking, but for some reason, I can't. I turn around and start to call after her, but pause. She's sitting back in the swing just watching me. "Yes?" she asks, almost mockingly.

I bite my lip, forcing all the mean quips I could throw at her back down. "You asked me this, so it's only fair that I ask you. Tell me, what is one thing that you would like to do?"

"That's easy," she answers immediately. "Just one night in London would do."

"I..." There's no way for me to respond, at least not appropriately, so I just nod and walk away.

Just one night in London. I can't help but smile, because that sounds like something my wife would have said. I can almost hear Jessica's voice superimposed over Tessa's statement. In fact, the statement seems almost familiar, but I can't place it. It hurts so much that I can't hold back the tears.

So, I don't. I just hope that I can clean it up before I find Pete. And I hope Pete is stocked up tonight.

Chapter Four
Blank Canvas

It truly is a blank canvas. The A.W.A Resource Center is a windowless, brick building that spans two stories. The front of the building is smooth and flat, and quite large. And by the positioning of the scaffolding, clearly where my work is to be displayed.

My work. That's something I never thought I would say again. But twenty-five thousand dollars up front was just too much to pass up. My addiction displayed my greed. And the one-hundred dollars Roman gave me didn't get very far with Pete. Once again, I'm having withdrawals and I need cash.

"You're late," a familiar voice says. I see Montica and her smooth ebony skin approaching me from the parking lot. She's like a foreign goddess, a girl I could use with no conviction, yet she is much more beautiful than the cheap women I've been buying lately. I know that thoughts like these are repulsive. They are thoughts that the old me would not think. Thoughts that I wish I could take away, but it's hard when I can only think of myself. "You were supposed to be here an hour ago."

"I start when I want to start, and a morning walk does well with design thoughts. Where's my check?"

Montica smiles. "You'll get it at the end of the day. It's coming from our main office in Rockville."

I feel my fists clench, but I let the tension flow out through my fingertips. I've suffered sobriety for longer than a day. I'll survive until the afternoon. I think.

Montica looks at me like I'm some type of hero. I've seen that look before from adoring fans. Usually strange art lovers and older rich folk. Never from a bald, dark-skinned, super-model-esque college student.

I know I can have her if I want her. She was strong with Bob, but I can see in her eyes that she's stricken.

She points to the building. "So, what do you think?"

"It's fine," I respond. Six months ago, I would have drooled over a project like this, money or no money. I can tell Montica doesn't know how to respond, so I do the talking. "So, what's your role?"

"I'm here for whatever you need—kind of like your assistant. And, as a direct support professional, I will be helping with a client who will be assisting—"

"Woah, woah, woah," I interrupt, placing my hand out in front of me. "I wasn't told I'd have a handicapped helper. That's only gonna slow me down. I don't need that."

That fire that Montica had with Bob flares within her eyes. "Not handicapped. Intellectually challenged, and quite the artist himself. His name is Ritchie, and he has Downs Syndrome. He will be helping as that's part of the deal. He was Roger's best friend, and since this memorial is about Roger, he will be a part of it. Do you want your money or not?"

I nod with clenched teeth. Stricken or not, these disabled people are a hot button for her.

"Good," she says. "Now, let's get a list of materials needed."

"That won't be necessary. It will take me at least the first two to three days just to design the project. All I need is a piece of paper and a pencil. And I need to meet my *helper* if you don't mind."

She smirks. "Yes, boss."

I spend the next twenty minutes standing in place and staring at the canvas in front of me. There is no inspiration at all. But I've never been a planner when it comes to art. I've just let my feelings do the work for me.

Whatever happens—happens. It's well documented in my work, and if Montica is really a fan of mine, then she saw right through my lie. She knows I'm stalling.

Jessica had become my muse when she was alive. But she's gone. I have nothing to inspire me now. Nothing.

When Montica returns, a short younger fellow with the clear appearance of Downs is following behind her. "Wesley, this is Ritchie. Ritchie, meet Wesley."

I shake his small, sweaty hand.

"Nice t-t-to... uh... m-meet you," he mumbles.

"Sure," I respond coldly, although he continues to smile.

"What... uh... can I... uh... d-do?" he asks.

I walk toward the building. "First off, stay out of my way. Second, tell me what you're good at. Montica seems to think you are good with art."

"I am good w-with p-p-painting. B-b-but I'm better... uh... w-with music."

"He's the lead singer of a rock band," Montica adds.

I laugh inside. This is some kind of joke. The kid can't even hardly put two words together. I bet his band of ret—as terrible a person as I am, I refuse to stoop to Bob's level on this one.

I put my hand on the brick wall. "Well, music isn't going to help me with this, so we'll stick to painting. I'm thinking iron bars and plywood." I turn to Montica, who is just staring at the building. "Are you writing this down princess?" Again, she's probably seeing right through me. I told her two to three days of planning and I'm already preparing supplies. But I can't just stand and stare at the wall for three days.

She snaps out of her daze and pulls out a piece of paper. "I thought you said you were just planning."

"I did, but now I'm inspired." Another lie, but iron and plywood is as good as anything else. And I figure Ritchie can't screw up painting either of them.

"This w-will be… uh… g-great. R-r-r-roger would be proud," Ritchie stammers.

I walk past the short man. "Don't get sentimental," I say. "We'll start the work tomorrow. I need the material by ten tomorrow morning."

"But we start at eight," Montica responds.

"I start at ten."

She bites back a retort. "Okay, how much material do you need?"

"It doesn't matter. Just get me some plywood and iron bars. And be prepared to go and buy more stuff tomorrow. I may change my mind."

Montica looks at Ritchie. "This is going to be something, isn't it?"

Ritchie nods. "Y-you are… uh… telling me." They both laugh.

I'm not laughing. "So, where is my check?"

"I told you it would be this afternoon. It's not even noon yet."

It's the end of the day for me. I have nothing left to do here. I'm already over this project. The faster I get it done, the better. I just can't find any reason within me to care for it. I used to love what I did. I can't feel that emotion with my work anymore. It's gone. Jessica took that with her.

"Well, then I'll have to get the check tomorrow. And you'll have to ask for the rest of the day off. I'll need someone to take me out tonight. I'll pay you back when I get paid."

Even with her dark skin, I can see the blush on her cheeks. "Well, my work is with you, so if you are done, then I guess I'll have to oblige you."

It's too easy. She's pathetic.

Montica puts her notepad into a small bag she has slung over her shoulder. She turns to Ritchie. "Go ahead and get back to your work inside. I'll see you tomorrow."

Ritchie waves like a little child, then turns and walks inside.

I grab Montica's hand and feign interest, lacing my fingers with hers. I'm sure this beautiful college student knows where the parties are at on Purdue's campus. There's sure to be several Pete-like characters there.

"Show me a good time," I tell her.

She giggles like a child, but I can tell she's a little hesitant, caught between her professional interests and her desire to please me.

So, I turn on the charm and pull her toward her car.

Chapter Five
Filth

Believe it or not, I was once the chivalrous type. I knew how to treat a woman with respect and dignity. I actually cared about people. I longed for love and hoped that it would be reciprocated.

That's not who I am today. I take what I want because I can. Because I have no other desire than to please myself. I live for me, for my addictions, for the numbness that comes with them. I do these things to keep from sobriety. What happens in the moments before I blackout are just unintended consequences. Collateral damage.

Last night, Montica was just collateral damage. She cried when I left her this morning. After I'd convinced her to get high with me. After I took advantage of her when she was not even herself. What girl can say she was able to sleep with her hero? Very few. But now she can.

That being said, she still cried this morning.

Before that, I remember crowds of college students dancing to dubstep beats. It felt like hours of ecstasy as we did lines of cocaine and boozed the night away. I don't know how much Montica paid the dealers last night. It must have been a small fortune. But she didn't seem to mind. She loved my attention. As the night wore on, she relished it.

But she still cried this morning.

"That was my first time," she whispered through tears as I got dressed. My heart sank as I turned toward the bed.

"I'm sorry."

"No, it's okay. I think I love you."

That was the booze and her loss of innocence talking. "No, you don't. You're not in your right mind. Get some coffee and Advil and I'll see you later today. You'll forget all about this."

I left, but not before I heard her whisper again. "But it was my first time."

That wasn't the first time I'd heard those words.

***

Jessica cries for several minutes. I try to comfort her, but there is nothing I can really do but hold her close. After a few moments of sobbing, she leans into my chest. "I'm sorry. I know we're married, and this should be a happy time. But this was my first time. I've saved myself for the man I was going to marry for so long, that it almost seems wrong to have done it. I just feel dirty."

I hug her tighter.

"I'm so sorry, this should be a happy time for us," *she repeats.*

"And it will be," I say. I push her away from me and lift her chin. I kiss the tears. "We'll take it slow. I promise. One night at a time."

She nods. "We do have forever."

"Forever," I repeat, before embracing her again.

***

For the first time in months, I feel regret for something I've done. At least for something I've done to a person. And as I sit here in my filthy house, it's not just Jessica's face that haunts my mind. It's Montica's too. Those tears gliding down her ebony skin tear a hole right through me. How terrible of a person am I, really?

The clock in the dining room chimes. Eleven times. I'm already an hour late. Looks like I'm going to start day two without showering, eating, or changing clothes.

There's a knock on my door. I cower, the loud sound ringing in my ears, much louder than it should. After the second knock I yell, "Hold on!"

I stumble to the door and open it, only to find a gun pointed at my face. It's Pete, and he looks angry.

Like any self-respecting person with a gun to their forehead, I raise my hands. For some reason, I immediately think of Tessa's words. She said that I didn't want to die. Right now, she's right. It's just like that dream of mine, that dream where I die with a bullet in my head contemplating happiness, but I'm not near as confident in real life. I back away from the doorway. "What's going on?"

Pete follows me in. His normally hipster appearance looks disheveled and greasy. "You went out and bought drugs from someone else last night." He places the gun against my forehead.

I feel my heart beating through my chest. In fact, it might just be knocking on the door behind Pete. Either that, or it's the wind knocking my screen door into the siding.

"We're not friends!" Pete yells. "I'm your dealer. I get you women, cocaine, and weed. What more can you ask for?" He pushes my head back with the cold barrel. "Never again. I have to support myself too, and Lafayette isn't the big city. I'll kill you if you use someone else. Understood?"

I nod, which is the scariest thing yet, feeling the gun push even harder against my skin.

"Good. Because you might be trying to kill yourself or whatever, but I have a family to take care of." He gives me one final shove with the gun, then walks out.

I take a breath and nearly fall over when he's out of sight. "So much for the only friend I have," I say aloud, if only to calm my nerves.

Pete might just be the death of me. I guess he supports my habit, and I support his family. Or, I guess, Roman has been.

It's ten after eleven now. But I need a drink before I can even think about working today.

***

I don't allow Joseph to see me. He's talking to Montica in front of the Resource Center. By the shaking of his head and the level of his voice, I know he's angry, and probably very disappointed with me. After my run-in with Pete this morning, I can't deal with another confrontation.

So, I wait for Joseph to leave before I step out from behind the corner of the building. The old curator has always looked out for me. He's always been my biggest fan. And besides Eliza and Roman, the one I've let down the most.

Montica bashfully smiles when she sees me. "A little late."

"Look, I'm sor—" I pause when I see Ritchie stacking full sheets of plywood. The little guy is handling them like they are cardboard. "Maybe he is going to be of some use."

Montica chuckles. "He'll surprise you a lot. Do you want your check? I'm guessing you won't be doing much work today since it's already noon."

She's clearly a mind reader, but first I have to mend what I did to her this morning. I grab her hands. "Look, I'm sorry about doing what I did to you last night. I took advantage of you."

"It's okay. I—"

"It's not," I interrupt. "Let me make it up to you by taking you out on a proper date." I'm not sure where this is coming from. The words leave my mouth faster than I can stop them. Everything I'm saying goes against how I actually feel. "Your choice."

Her smile spans ear to ear. "Saturday. Ritchie has a concert. His band is playing downtown."

I should make up an excuse now—anything. "Deal." *What am I doing?*

She blushes.

"Now, let's get that check. You're right, I'm not doing anything today."

She doesn't even question me. "Come on, I'll introduce you to my boss. She has your money."

I follow her inside. Ritchie waves as I pass. "H-hi."

I nod, still unsure how the small Downs boy is so strong, or how he sings with his stutter. Maybe he will surprise me.

Inside, the A.W.A Resource Center is in chaos. The staff chase after screaming adults and one member stands separating a group of girls who were hitting each other in the corner of the main entrance. The building is very cozy, and the crazy that ensues looks unnaturally superimposed on the calm background.

Montica doesn't seem fazed by any of it, whereas I'm dodging blows and clutching my ears. "We specialize in high behavior individuals, as well as training high-functioning persons like Ritchie."

"Now Angela, what is the right thing to do?" a young woman asks in a very motherly tone as she holds the hand of a smaller girl, who is drooling out of the side of her mouth.

"Hi," the girl says. Then repeats the word over and over, waving her other hand in the air.

Montica takes me through a door, and the more rooms I pass, the more convinced I am that this used to be a medical facility that was converted into a place for the disabled—and clearly some mentally challenged people as well. Montica would despise my thought process, so I keep it to myself.

When we reach the office and Montica closes the door, the silence is amazing. I need a hit after that mess. My nerves are on end—I'd rather have Pete's gun again.

Sitting at a desk is a woman, hovering over a small boy. She talks to him in hushed tones as he writes something on the paper.

"Long time no see," Tessa says, looking up and completely catching me off-guard.

Montica looks back between the both of us. "You know each other?"

I thought I'd never see her again after that botched dinner at Roman and Eliza's. I nod. "One night in London."

Tessa smirks. Montica gives me her best confused look.

"So, this is your new job?"

"Yes, it is," Tessa answers. "Well, not necessarily new. I started nearly six months ago."

The paper beneath the boy's pencil, it's a picture of a waterfall spraying over rocks. Not just any picture, but a masterpiece—something that should be hung up in the gallery.

"This is Anthony," Tessa says. "He doesn't speak, but he is an artist."

"Hi, Anthony."

The boy doesn't look up and instead continues to draw.

"You're here for your money, I suppose?" Tessa asks. She walks over to another desk against the wall and opens up a drawer. "Here you go." She places the check in my hand.

I look at it, twenty-five thousand dollars typed on the paper with my name as the payee.

Tessa leans closer to me. "Don't break her heart," she says. I follow her gaze to Montica, who is now leaning over Anthony and whispering gently.

"I'm sure I will. Anyway, I'm done for the day boss. I'll get started tomorrow."

Tessa's expression doesn't change. "Two days and you haven't done a thing. I would have fired you yesterday. But Joseph seems to think you'll do a great job."

"He's an idiot."

"And so are you," Tessa responds. "Now, I've actually got work that I *have* to get done, so if you'll excuse me."

I put the check in my pocket and turn to leave.

"Oh, and Wes, try not to waste too much of Montica's time. The fact that I can't use her as direct support is hard enough with my current staffing."

She's talking about work, but for some reason, I can't help but feel that part of it still has to do with not breaking her heart. She's like my mother. Just like her.

I nod and leave. Tessa seems a little more like 'one day in hell' than 'one night in London.' Maybe that's just my headache talking. I know how to take care of that.

Chapter Six
Artwork

"You're early," Joseph says with a grin, as he looks at his watch. He's leaning casually against his Mercedes-Benz outside the Resource Center.

As if you're not waiting to check up on me. I walk past him. "Well, don't go crying about it."

"You smell like alcohol."

"You smell like old man cologne. What does it matter?"

Joseph smiles. "I guess it doesn't. I'm just glad to see you are taking the job somewhat seriously. Jessica would be proud."

I stop. "No, she wouldn't be. Look at me. I wore this yesterday. I haven't showered, and I'm hungover." And what he doesn't know is that I bought a bottle of whiskey yesterday. But no drugs. I cashed a twenty-five thousand dollar check, and all I bought was one bottle. Don't get me wrong, it knocked me out, which is exactly what the doctor ordered.

But I didn't see Pete. I just couldn't find it within myself to give money to a man that had put a gun in my face that morning. I almost succumbed to my addiction, but every time the temptation was too much, I just drank more. I stood in the doorway of our bedroom, staring at that forsaken letter, Jessica's last words. And when I couldn't look at it anymore, I drank more. That is, until all went black. I welcomed the darkness like an old friend.

I woke up with my face on the dirty dining room table, a pounding headache, surrounded by one-hundred dollar bills. Every addict's dream, minus the headache of course.

I left the money on the table.

He opens his door. "Don't be so hard on yourself. Believe it or not, I thought you would bolt as soon as you got the check. I'm happy you didn't."

The glint of a tear sparkles in his eyes. Just like him to be proud of me even in this state of existence.

I wave him away. "Just go before you cry."

He nods before getting into his car. He doesn't leave immediately and instead rolls down his window. "You're wrong. She would've been proud."

I turn to my work, pretending to ignore him. His tears are enough. He doesn't need to see mine. I wait until he is gone before wiping my face. He doesn't know what he is talking about. How could she be proud of this?

It doesn't matter. She's gone.

After a few minutes, I pick up the hammer and slam it against the metal sheet, my first art project in six months. I thought it would hurt worse, but I really don't feel anything. It's like riding a bike.

Though I still can't find the inspiration for this piece, I know I was born for this.

***

Sweat drips off my forehead and I'm pretty sure I can smell last night's whiskey as it exits my pores. *Poor Ritchie.* We finish hanging the second metal pipe, held together by plastic zip-ties right now. This heat, mixed with my hangover, has me spent.

"Let's call it a day, Ritchie. I'll have to get a welder to finish it, anyway."

I have no idea where I'm going with the piece. I stand in the front lawn of the Resource Center just staring up at the monstrosity of brick that still has to be covered.

"Are w-we p-p-painting it?" Ritchie asks.

It's gonna need a lot more than paint. "Not yet," I say.

"Hi," a weak voice says from behind me.

I turn to see the girl from yesterday, the one who had the staff guide her by hand. Angela, if I remember correctly. She's small, with short-cropped brown hair, and deep inset eyes that seem to look off in the distance.

I nod.

"Hi," she repeats, still not looking at me.

"Hello," I say, a little unnerved.

"Hi."

"There you are," says another voice. It's the same staff-woman from yesterday. "I'm so sorry, Mr. Gerhard."

"It's okay," I assure her. "What's wrong with her?"

The woman looks at me in disgust before grabbing the girl's hand. She whispers something in her ear and they walk away, but not before the girl says "hi" several more times.

I feel eyes behind me.

"There is nothing wrong with her," Montica says. "She was born with autism, MR, and a host of other medical issues. 'Hi' is the only word she knows. I've been here for a year and a half and I've never heard her say anything else. She used to say other words, or so I'm told, but that seems to be more myth than fact at this point."

I turn to see Montica in her best goddess form, the sheen of sweat on her dark skin. She's wearing a black tank top and jeans, which only accentuates her model-like figure. "Where have you been?"

"Helping inside for a moment."

"You're supposed to be helping me."

She rolls her eyes. "I'm here now."

"Well, me and Ritchie are done. Let's call it a day."

Ritchie sighs.

"Do you think Roger would like our progress?" I ask.

Ritchie shakes his head and smiles. "Of c-course."

"That's all I need to hear." I wave at him. "I'll see you tomorrow."

Montica grabs my arm before I can walk away. She holds on tightly, and I can tell that she's waiting for Ritchie to go inside before she speaks. Once the main door closes, she sheepishly looks at me. "This date on Saturday... is it for real or are you just trying to make up for what happened? I mean, you taking my... and my crying... well, you know." She turns away embarrassed.

I put my other hand around her waist. "Can't a guy take out a beautiful woman?" I'm lying. I'm doing it for the exact reasons she just stated. I'm doing it for my own conscience. Not for her.

She smiles, then pecks me on the cheek. "Okay. I'm sorry for being so awkward," she says close to my ear. She shouldn't be sorry for anything. I should be.

I brush her lips with mine. "We shouldn't do this at work."

She pulls away, blushing. "You're probably right."

As if my conscience wasn't being pricked enough by the vision of her crying the other night, her outright naivety to my lies just makes it worse. I pull away from her and start walking toward the street.

"I can give you a ride if you want?" she calls after me.

"I'm fine." Another lie. If I was fine, I wouldn't feel so bad for stringing her along.

I'm so pathetic. In a way, my lies are just like this art project. I've started with two iron pipes and two lies. Both will keep growing until they become an entity all to themselves. Both have lasting consequences.

And both I have the ability to fix.

The question is, will I?

Chapter Seven
Into the Pit

Yesterday, I had a brief bout with my conscience. Today, I couldn't care less. It was another hot day—the Indiana type of hot. The kind of hot that needs to end with a downer.

The alcohol isn't enough. I need something stronger.

So, I'm going to see Pete.

It's getting dark out, a minor relief from the constant heat of the sun. Ritchie and I managed two more bars today, and some messed up plywood design that looks like it came straight out of a horror movie. It will have to be fixed. I don't know where I'm going with the piece, but right now, it's not in the right direction.

Like I said, I've never been one to plan my art, but I used to get good feelings from it. I used to feel pleasure from the junk pieces I put together. But this is just a job. To Montica and Ritchie and everyone else involved with the project, it is much more. To me, it's a means to an end.

Pete lives in an apartment complex just off Third Street, about a twenty-minute walk from my house. It's an old area of town, beat down by years of time and a horde of less-than-caring residents. It's a rough place to go, but if I get my fix, it's clearly worth it. Before she died, I would have never come this way. I would have been afraid to.

I see Pete long before I reach the complex. He's sitting on a small piece of cracked cement that goes for a deck. His wife, Alexandra, sits across from him; one of those old glass porch tables is placed between them. Even from here, I can already see the band around her arm and the needles strewn out on the table.

There is no shame here. Even the cops ignore this area. If I did this on my front porch, I'd have already been arrested months ago.

When he sees me, Pete yells at her. "Get inside, woman!"

She moans something, then gathers up her paraphernalia and walks through the sliding door that doubles as a front door.

"Well, it looks like you decided to listen to me."

"Not by choice," I answer. "Just hook me up."

Pete wryly grins. "I should have guessed you'd start to go straight when that woman kicked me out of your house a couple of weeks ago. If it wasn't for her body, I might have done a little damage to her, you know."

I sit down where Alexandra was moments earlier. "That woman is my sister-in-law. And you can threaten me, but don't threaten my family."

"What family?" Pete asks. "Didn't your family die earlier this year?"

If it were any other person, I might have punched him in the face. But Pete is a terrible person, the scum of the earth. I wouldn't dare dignify his cold words with a reaction, even if they do sting immensely.

"Forget it," he says, clearly noticing whatever expression the pain of his words causes me, even if subtle. His apology is hollow and merely a formality. "What can I get you?"

"The usual."

"Do you want a woman too?" he asks.

"No."

Pete laughs as he stands up. "Why, because of that woman that bought drugs for you the other night?"

I don't answer. Pete snarls then goes inside. I hear him yelling profanities, Alexandra spitting them back, and a child crying. I'm disgusted by it all. Yet here I am, dealing with a man who perpetuates this filth.

I've called Pete my friend from time to time, but really, he's nothing to me. He's one step away from being my enemy, and one step away from becoming my murderer.

"Here you go," Pete says, interrupting my thoughts. He throws two baggies on the table, one marijuana, the other cocaine. "Now pay up."

I pull the cash out of my pocket.

"And it will be a ten percent increase since you tried to go elsewhere."

I don't even look up as I hand over an extra hundred dollars. I grab the drugs and leave. But Pete isn't done talking yet.

"Hey, I know you've got yourself a job now," he calls after me.

I turn around just as one of his kids peeks out the window. Pete calls the small blonde-haired boy a name that no child should be called and tells him to go inside. The boy is gone as quickly as he appeared.

"So?" Pete asks, his attention back on me.

"Yeah, that's where I got my money. I don't need to borrow it from my family anymore."

Pete's expression grows dim. He looks a lot like the way he did when he had his gun pointed to my face. "You're not really thinking about going straight are you?"

"And if I was?"

I see a quick flash of anger, but then he grins. "You'll never change. You're just like me, and you always will be. If it wasn't for your wife's death, a divorce or something else would have driven you right to this life. You want the drugs. You need them."

There are words to counter his argument, but I can feel the drugs in my hand, and the sense of relief that comes along with them.

"No, I would never treat my family like you do, Pete."

He laughs, while placing a cigarette in his mouth. "You already do. You've shunned them. And I've seen how you treat your women. I'm sure you've already used up that pretty little black girl."

The sting of my conscience pricks me. He's right on all counts. I took Montica's innocence like it was mine in the first place. And I have completely shut out the people that love me most.

"What's the matter? You know I'm right, don't you?" Pete callously laughs.

I shake my head. "Maybe, but not for long. I'll prove you wrong someday."

His laughter continues, the cigarette shaking between his lips. "Spoken like a true crack head. Someday. In a few years. Tomorrow." He shoos me away with his right hand. "Go on and do your best. But you'll be back here kissing my feet in few days."

I have nothing more to say. The realization that I am nothing better than Pete is hard to swallow. Take the most worthless piece of crap in the city, and I'm his equal.

But I have my drugs. My god. My everything.

Isn't that what's important?

As I walk away, I try to tell myself that I am nothing like him. Over and over I say the words, but there is no conviction behind them. I don't know how Pete became this way—a drug dealing domestic abuser—but I know where I once was. And I have opportunities to change.

My thoughts are interrupted by a ring on my new cell phone. Another perk of my windfall of cash. Montica's name flashes across the screen. This is one of those opportunities where I can be different.

I can make up for stealing Montica's innocence. I can show her that I'm not like Pete.

"Hello."

"Hi, it's me."

"Yeah, I know. You're the only person I gave my number to."

I can hear the embarrassment in her laugh. "I just wanted to make sure about tomorrow. Our date."

"Ritchie's concert is at seven, right?" I know the answer.

"Yeah."

"Then pick me up at five-thirty. A man can't take a woman out without food."

"Okay, will do." I can sense how excited she is.

I'm not. There was one woman in my life. And God took her away from me. If it wasn't for the fact that I'm trying to do right by Montica, I wouldn't be doing this at all. I can thank Pete for arousing this do-good behavior.

"I'll see you tomorrow."

"Definitely. Bye."

I put the phone back in my pocket. Going to this concert sounds like a terrible idea. I can't even imagine Ritchie stuttering through his lyrics on stage. Well, I can, and I'm embarrassed for him already.

I feel the drugs in my pocket again. At least I'll be able to forget about all of this tonight.

Chapter Eight
Goodnight to You and Your Friends

Every part of me wanted to run from tonight. I had a full day to grasp my situation, so I drank most of it away, but left some time to sober up a little before my date with Montica. For the first time in six months, save my meeting at the Art Studio, I put on something nice. Some dress pants and a polo shirt. After a quick glance in the mirror, I realized I looked like Roman, except a much smaller version. The pale, skinny version who looks like he's been on a bender for months. Because he has.

My palms were sweaty when she pulled up to the house. I took one more shot of whiskey and walked out to meet her. If she was nervous, she didn't show it.

I got my first real glance at Montica when we entered the restaurant, a small little place in West Lafayette, near Purdue's campus. Having seen her body close up, I knew she was beautiful, but tonight was different. She wore a yellow dress with strapped sandals. She looked every bit a college student, but also every bit a woman. It was hard to take my eyes off her.

But she's still not Jessica. It took me months to find the courage to ask my wife out for the first time. I was enthralled by her golden hair, her blue eyes, her calming smile. And scared of her clear superiority to me. But after much encouragement from Joseph, I was able to ask her to coffee.

I fell in love hard. We were married not five months later.

That was a lifetime ago, or at least it feels as much. In all honesty, it was only three years ago.

I may have betrayed myself while my mind compared the two women, but Montica never asked me why my eyes became so watery during our meal. Thankfully, she didn't ask me much at all, and instead carried the conversation with talk of her summer plans and her work with the disabled—I mean special needs.

I nodded my way through the entire meal, my mind lost in memories of times when my wife would sit across from me and talk for hours, and I would just listen, because the sound of her voice was enough. That is, until things got bad. But I don't delve into the bad, because it's the sound of her voice, the stirring of her emotions, and the clear motivation in Jessica's actions that I've lost. It's those things that I can never get back. It's those things that I fell in love with in the first place.

"Well, I think it's time we should go. The concert starts in twenty minutes."

I glance at my phone and pretend to be looking at the time. "Sounds good to me." I wave at the waiter.

Montica puts her hand on mine. "It's okay, I already paid for the meal a while ago."

I do my best to look embarrassed and upset at myself. "I'm sorry, it's just my attention span is well—"

"No," she interrupts, "I'm sorry for completely hogging the entire conversation. You're probably tired of listening to me talk." She sheepishly looks down at the table.

I flip over my hand so hers is resting on my palm. "It's okay, I'm not very good at this." I hold on to her hand as I stand up. "I'll try to be a little more engaged for the rest of the night."

She laughs. "Well, a rock concert probably isn't the best place to try to be more engaged."

She's right. In my mind, though, it's the perfect place for me to disengage and finish tonight out.

I half expected we would end up at some coffee house or church event, where a bunch of nice people would show up to support the local *special* kid and his band of misfits. So, when we walked into the smoky bar, my mind did a double take–Ritchie, in his blue jeans and white t-shirt standing on the battered stage tuning an electric guitar. He was surrounded by a group of tattooed individuals with long hair, piercings, and dark clothes, and he looked completely out of his element.

"Let's sit over here," Montica says, pulling me toward the bar. There are two empty seats crammed in between the masses.

I fall into the seat and immediately grab the attention of the bartender.

"What can I get ya?" the balding man asks.

"I'll take a water," Montica says before I can answer.

I look at her in question.

"I'm going to try to be a good role model for Ritchie," she says. "And I'd like to remember this date, unlike the last time we went out."

Her words are sharp, which is more than enough reason for me to do the opposite. "Give me two shots of whiskey. I'm going to drink for her tonight."

He smiles. "Starting a tab?"

I nod. "Just keep them coming."

I can tell Montica is trying to ignore my self-destructive behavior. One of the other guitar players is warming up, which causes the crowd to cheer, and means I don't have to worry about carrying on a conversation.

Then I see Tessa down on the end of the bar, her dress slacks and teacher sweater making her stick out like a sore thumb. She smiles back at me, then turns away. For some reason, I have a strong desire to go and talk to her, but my whiskey arrives just in time to kill that idea.

"Here they go," Montica yells through the noise.

I down one shot and follow her eyes to the stage. I can't help but feel embarrassed for Ritchie already. He steps up to the mic with his Down features front and center. I can almost hear his stuttering before he even starts to speak.

"Get ready for the surprise of your life," Montica shouts.

Feedback makes the crowd grow silent. The rest of Ritchie's band, which I assume is called The Forgotten by the large banner behind them, steps into place. They look like they are ready to melt some faces, which makes the sight of Ritchie superimposed in between them even more confusing.

"I w-would l-l-like to think all of y-you f-f-for… for… coming," Ritchie stammers through his introduction.

Even so, cheers fly his way, from young adult metal-heads to middle-aged men and women. Montica yells and claps with them. I take my next shot of whiskey and nod for the bartender to bring me more.

"As s-some of y-you know, w-we always s-s-start with this s-song," Ritchie continues.

Someone in the crowd yells out something. The crowd cheers.

Ritchie smiles. "What w-was that?"

In a chorus of screams, I hear the song title. "Goodnight to You and Your Friends."

Ritchie strikes a chord on his guitar, and I can feel the vibration surging through my chest. He yells, without stuttering at all. "Goodnight to You and Your Friends!"

And for the next hour, I feel like I'm alone, watching a miracle.

***

Ritchie didn't stutter one time for the remainder of the night. The boy that I order around all day was a guitar god, playing guitar solos and screaming out lyrics with a voice stolen from Axl Rose, who by the way is another destructive soul from the Lafayette area.

The rest of the band was good. Ritchie was great.

I was so enthralled with the talent of my *special* acquaintance that I had neglected the last shot of whiskey the bartender brought. I then felt Montica's eyes glued to me, and I knew one of those I-told-you-so expressions was on her face.

But I can't argue with the fact that she was right. I was so wrong. There was nothing really wrong with Ritchie. His Down syndrome made him appear different, but he wasn't. He was just like me. But his struggles were not by his own doing. And he didn't let those struggles keep him from his art, his passion.

My struggles were all me, with a little help from the man upstairs. I mean, it wasn't me that took her away. But I was choosing to live like Pete. I was being Pete, completely clinging to the bottom of the well, letting everything I'd ever loved leave me, as if my beautiful wife took it all with her when she died.

Something in me clicked. Montica said something about wanting to say hi to Ritchie, but I pulled her out of that bar as fast as I could.

I managed to wave at Ritchie before I left. He was talking to Tessa just in front of the stage.

And for the rest of the night, I treated Montica like she deserved to be treated. Like a person, not an obstacle.

Now, it's nearing midnight. Montica looks at me from across her apartment's dining room table. "What is with you tonight? When I picked you up, you didn't seem to care less about our date. Now, you won't stop talking."

It's true. I'd told her stories about my past life, my triumphs, and things that skimmed the edge of hurting me. I stopped just short of talking about Jessica.

"I'm inspired," I respond, sipping on coffee. I need a hit, but two or three cups of caffeine will have to do.

Montica slides into the chair beside me before running her fingers through my hair. "Seeing Ritchie will do that. I'm sure when you first heard about this job, you looked at these people like Bob does. Like the little retard kids at the special school. But that's not it at all. They are normal people. They have abilities."

"Don't lump me into the same category as Bob." It's bad enough being like Pete. I don't need another chauvinistic pig added to my resume. Of course, the way I treat the women Pete gets me is suspect.

Montica's soft fingers glide down to my chin, and then my neck. Her dark ebony skin is aglow with the moonlight that shines through the kitchen window and into the attached dining area. "You're already changing in a week."

She sounds like Tessa.

Why has my conscience awakened? I don't like it. And I don't like how even when this beautiful woman touches me, I still have a place in the back of my mind begging for drugs. Even with the inspiration of Ritchie's music, I still have a desire for the burn of alcohol. Even with the love of my family, I still feel hopeless.

"I hope you're right," I say.

"This *you* is how I imagined my idol would be. I imagined you to be caring and compassionate, and not egotistical. I could see it in your art. It's why I always wanted to be an artist. But then I met you a few weeks ago. And you were everything I didn't think you would be. But I see some of what I imagined in there."

I touch her face. "Again, I hope you're right."

She kisses me.

And for a moment, I forget all of my troubles in the passion of a young woman.

She releases her lips. "Do you want to stay the night?"

I can think of nothing better.

Chapter Nine
Inspired

I feel Jessica beside me. Her beautiful blue eyes rest on my face, somehow seeing the love of her life in me. Her blond hair tickles my arm, but I don't dare move.

"I think it worked this time. I can feel it."

I laugh. "How many times have you said that before?"

She giggles, nudging her body closer to mine. "Every time I believe."

"And what have I said every time?"

She sighs, but I can still feel her smile next to me. "Be patient, don't stress, and it will happen. And I'm really trying you know. I just want you to love me forever. And I'm afraid you won't if I can't give you this."

I turn and look at her face. I kiss her soft lips. "Even if you never gave me anything else, I would love you. But I'm not worried. God will give us this."

She smiles, but there are tears in her eyes, as if she senses that I'm lying.

***

What if I was lying? I left God a long time ago. She was always the one with the blind faith. I guess I was a follower in that sense.

Either way, there's a brief moment that I feel my wife beside me. In the dark, I feel the warmth of another, but the dark skin tells me that it's not her. After a few seconds, the realizations pour in again. Jessica is gone. Dead.

This woman beside me is nothing more than a fling—a pipe dream. She thinks I can change. And maybe for a time I can believe her, but I know that the pull of my current lifestyle will suck me in. Even God can't seem to pull me out of this mess that I'm in. And He sure can't bring Jessica back. He can't erase what He's already done.

I see Ritchie in my head, the rock god of legend. His image is replaced by the shoddy artwork I'm placing on the front of his building—Roger's building. Every day he comes to help me for the sake of this special man I've never met, his best friend. Who was this Roger? What made him so special?

It's dark, but I'm completely awake. And I can't stay here. Normally, there would only be one option. Find Pete. But for some reason, I feel inspired to do something that I haven't done in a long time. I can thank Ritchie for this stray thought.

I can almost see Jessica's smile again as my mind races. I pull myself out of the bed, trying not to disturb Montica. I hope she knows I'm not leaving her like a one-night stand victim. I'll leave a note. That's the least I can do for the wonderful night she gave me.

Fifteen minutes later and I'm walking down Main Street. A block away, I see the studio. The Art Studio at night reminds me of myself. It's well-lit and alive in the darkness. But inside, nothing stirs.

There's a window in the back that I can sneak into. I'd done it many times in my heyday, much to Bob and Joseph's chagrin. I pass Eliza's antique shop on the way, which reminds me that Eliza and Roman are having a baby. Images of them leaning over a cradle singe my brain and I want to be happy for them, but I'm not. I will certainly be the worst uncle to have ever lived. I can't be happy, not for this.

The smell of paint and other art materials pulls me from my reverie as I slide through the window and step into the dark, quiet building. Light shines from Bob's office, but I know it's only his lamp. Bob never works more than he has to. The fat pig barely works at all. If not for Joseph, this studio would have gone under a long time ago. In fact, and I say this without ego, my fame had a big part in keeping the doors open too. Well, and Bob's money. His never-ending supply.

Now that my eyes are adjusted, I walk through the main gallery, careful to keep my eyes away from the front desk. If I look at it, I will see Jessica's ghostly outline sitting behind the old wooden counter, a greeting forming on her lips.

My office welcomes me with dust and cobwebs. There's a stack of mail on the floor. I push it over to the side with my foot. Once my bearings are straight, I sit behind the messy desk. The unfinished piece calls for my hands. There's still a pair of wire cutters next to the barbed wire wrapped around the pole. The wire pools on the floor to the left of my desk. I remember picking it up from an old church acquaintance. A nice old farmer that Jessica had taken to—like everyone she met. He was a man of faith. What would he think of me now? I haven't stepped foot in a church building since the funeral. Like I said, God and I aren't quite on the same page right now.

Jessica would have hated this part of me. My hatred for the God that she so loved.

I shake the thoughts from my head and remember Ritchie and his greatness. He's the reason I'm here. My current inspiration. The only thing keeping me from Pete.

I grab the wire cutters and place the ends around the barbed wire. It's like this small piece has been waiting, frozen in time for this very moment. Just like me, frozen in a purgatory-like madness.

With a firm squeeze, the wire separates into two entities. One end falls to the floor, the other snags on the desk and becomes a permanent part of an art piece that until two minutes ago had no future.

There's a feeling that floods inside of me, one that I haven't felt since I last worked on this piece, over six months ago. The feeling is genuine pleasure—pleasure in the work of art at the tip of my fingers. Pleasure in the molding of this junk into something far more. Pleasure in creativity.

I haven't felt any of this while working on the piece for the Resource Center. No, I've just placed pieces up on a wall in random movements.

There's been a great disservice done to this Roger character, and to those whom he called friends. A great disservice. Fifty thousand dollars and I can't even force myself to be half as inspired on that project as I am tonight.

My hands go to work, pulling out more wire into straight lines. I put on gloves to keep from cutting myself. My tools are all where I remember them. It's like I've never left. Nothing feels more right than a welding mask and the flame of my mini-welder. I remember when Bob and Joseph both demanded I not have an open flame in my office. But after I made them millions of dollars, they stopped being so demanding. That, and they supposedly hired some specialist to fireproof the exterior of my office.

I don't know how long I've been working, but at some point, I decided to add small railroad spikes wrapped with the rusty wire. There's a design in there somewhere. I can almost see it in my head, but I have to put it together to bring out the full picture. That's how it's always been. Like I've said before, I'm not a planner. I never will be.

It might have been thirty minutes. It might have been hours. I'm not sure. But Joseph appears in my office doorway. He clears his throat, and I note his pajama pants and slippers beneath a black windbreaker jacket. I stop working and look at him. He has tears in his eyes. *Sentimental fool.*

"How long have you been here?"

He smiles. "Well, since you tripped the silent alarm six hours ago. But I didn't want to stop your work. I thought an animal had tripped the alarm or something. I couldn't believe my eyes."

Six hours. I step away from the art piece in front of me. It no longer resembles what was on my desk earlier.

"Good thinking on putting an alarm in," I say. "So why are you interrupting me now? I think I'm about finished."

Joseph's smile disappears. "Now, don't get too upset. It's not serious." He steps out of the doorway where Tessa is waiting behind him, she too in sleep attire. Sweat pants and a long sleeve shirt.

She gives me a weak smile. "Roman and Eliza have been trying to get a hold of you for hours. They finally called me, thinking I'd have an idea, since I've seen you more lately than they have. So, I called Joseph, who happened to be here with you."

"What's wrong?" I immediately ask. Nausea sets in at the thought of Eliza's pregnancy.

"It's your mom."

"But like I said," Joseph follows, putting his hands out. "She's fine. She just—"

I'm already pushing them out of the way. "Where is she?"

"St. Elizabeth Central."

That's not very far from the Studio. I could get there running in ten minutes. I stop in the hallway, my mind telling me what a ridiculous idea that is. I'm so used to doing things on my own. I turn, and Tessa is right behind me.

"I'm parked out front." She grabs my arm and pulls me with her.

Chapter Ten
To Die Happy

"She collapsed helping a friend in her garden. Heat exhaustion. But they think she'll be fine, they just want to check her heart due to her history of heart attacks." Tessa squeezes my forearm.

She's had three heart attacks in the last ten years. Overexertion usually the cause. It's just like my mother to spend her time helping others while killing herself. Clearly, I didn't get much of the "helping" gene from her. I think my womb-mate, Roman, stole all of that.

"She's a master manipulator. She faked a heart attack once, just to get the family together. It wouldn't surprise me if she did this just to get to me. I wouldn't put it past her."

"You can't blame her. The last time she tried to see you all she saw was your back as you ran away into the night."

"Are you serious?"

Tessa shrugs, a tired grin on her face. "I would do anything to see Kalen."

I want to argue, but there's no point. I don't want to talk. Thankfully, Tessa stays silent the rest of the way.

St. Elizabeth Central isn't far from the Studio. About a three-minute drive through central Lafayette. Tessa pulls up to the main entrance and parks the car, but doesn't shut off the ignition.

"Good luck."

"Wait, where are you going?"

"What do you mean? I'm going back home and sleeping. I've been up far too long."

I grab her arm. "Please, come in with me."

She shakes her head. "I'm not a part of your family. I don't belong in there. Call Montica or something." Her mention of Montica sounds more like a scolding than a suggestion.

"But you're already awake. Please, I need support to face my family."

Tessa sighs, then turns the car off. "Are you serious?"

"It wouldn't be the first time you've been asked to do something for me. Right?"

"And I'm guessing not the last. And for the record, this is actually the third time." She's obstinate, but her body language doesn't seem to convey much of a struggle.

I give her my best smile. I'm not even sure why I want her to go in with me. For all intents and purposes, she's my boss, and she's Roman and Eliza's last attempt at relating to me. Normally, she would've been the last person I'd want to be with. But there's just something about her. Maybe it's her calm presence. Maybe it's because she reminds me of Jessica. She has black hair and green eyes, the opposite of my wife's blonde and blue. But I can't help seeing her. Maybe it's the willingness to help, the concern. I don't know.

We find Eliza and Roman just inside the main entrance. Both of them look exhausted, but force a smile when I walk through the door. Eliza immediately wraps her thin arms around me. "I'm glad she found you."

I awkwardly hug her back. "How's Mom?"

"She's absolutely fine," Roman responds, a hint of annoyance in his voice. "Apparently, she tripped and landed on her knee hard. I guess that is what she is now calling 'collapsing.'"

I shake my head. *Manipulation.*

"Hi, Tessa. Thanks for your help. So sorry to drag you into our business."

I bite my tongue.

"It's no problem," she responds, grabbing Eliza's hand in both of hers.

Roman puts his hand on my shoulder with a firm grip. "She's in room 209. Don't tell her that we're on to her games. And just be nice."

"Wait, where are you going?"

"We've been here for two hours," Eliza says. "We'll wait for you out here. Technically, visiting hours were over about eight hours ago, but Roman knows a guy who knows a guy."

Just like him. I look to Tessa. "She's going to take me home," I say. Eliza and Roman both start to object, but Tessa interrupts them and answers contrary to what I see in her expression. "It's fine. I'll take him home."

I can see the desire in Eliza's eyes to say more, but Roman grabs her hand. She complies and starts to walk away.

"Wait," I call after them. "Eliza, I... " The words are hard to find. "Congrats on the baby." I barely get the last word out of my mouth before a deep pain in my stomach forms. I turn and walk away before she can respond.

When I'm around the corner—and I've stopped a nurse to ask where 209 is—I practically run to the room. My dad is just inside, his short, stocky frame capped off by salt and pepper hair, a little more salt than I remember. He's sitting at the end of the bed, his face buried in his laptop. He doesn't even look up when I walk in.

"Hey... Dad."

His head doesn't move, but his eyes peer in my direction. He smiles. "Your mother has been waiting for you."

"He's here?" My mother questions from the other side of a floral-patterned curtain.

"Yes, I'm here." I walk into her line of sight, and immediately she has her arms outstretched for an embrace.

I comply. She squeezes tightly and practically pulls me onto the bed. "I'm so happy you're here."

I pry myself away. "Sorry it took so long."

"Almost seven months," she says. Her soft eyes begin to tear up. She too, looks like she's aged since the funeral. Her long, dark hair seems lighter. Her eyes seem dimmer.

"I meant tonight. The last seven months have been on purpose," I say coldly.

She turns the faucet on in full force. "I hate to agree with you, but I'm sure Jessica is worth the pain and sorrow you've thrown on yourself," she says. "But I don't think the life you are leading now is how she would have wanted you to carry it. If you'd just let God—"

"Me and God aren't on good terms."

I feel my dad's arm on my shoulder, just like Roman would do. It's a trait passed down in our family, another one that I've strayed from. "Mary, let's just be happy that he's here."

She nods. "Yes, now I can die happy."

"You're not dying Mom."

She smiles. "Each day I have to fret about you, I die a little more."

"We both do," Dad adds.

"I'm sorry." I don't have anything else to say. I've run from them, hidden the life that I lead all because I don't want them to see me like this, but it's futile. They see me.

"Please, tell me you didn't do this on purpose."

"Of course not," she says, overly exaggerating her surprise at such a question.

"If I promise to visit soon, will you be more careful?"

She nods vigorously.

"That's all we want," my dad says. "When we missed you at your brother's house the other day, it hurt terribly."

I allow my shoulders to fall. "I'm sorry. I really am."

"Don't be. Just allow us back into your life. It sounds like you are doing better, and we want to be here with you as you get your life back on track."

I don't tell them that my plan for the rest of the night—what little is left—is to get drunk and high, and hope that I wake up tomorrow. If that's getting my life back on track, then I must be doing well.

***

Tessa's waiting in the lobby when I return just as she promised, her chin resting on her hands, her elbows on her knees. She yawns just before she sees me.

"Thanks for waiting."

"It's fine," she says. But she's not fine. I can see it in her eyes. She's annoyed and tired. I'm not sure why she gave into my request—well, demand—but I am grateful.

Even though morning is just around the corner, and I'm sure that she's frustrated with how her night has gone, Tessa still finds humor in the situation. She opens the passenger side door and waves me inside. "Your taxi service, my good sir."

"Thanks," I respond politely. "You make an excellent boss."

"I'm not your boss," she says once she's in the car. "I oversee the site you happen to be doing a project at. I'm your friend."

"Right. The one who's been through what I have. That's what you told me at Columbian Park a few weeks back."

"And you said that you didn't want to hear about it." She pulls away from the curb.

"Yeah, about that… " I start. I really shouldn't have to apologize since she was the one that chased after me. And the only reason we even met was because Eliza and

Roman meddled. But then again, she did help me tonight. She is helping still. "… I was a jerk. I'm sorry."

She laughs. Just like she did when I told her I wanted to die in the park that night. Finally, after a few moments, she puts her hand over her mouth. "I'm sorry for laughing. I just didn't think you had that in you."

"Me neither."

We drive for a few minutes in the general direction of my house before she turns down South Street and starts driving in the opposite direction.

"Where are you going? Do you know where I live?"

"I do," she says. "Which is why I'm not taking you there."

"Wait. What?"

She puts her hand on my arm. "Just answer me this. What would you do if I took you home right now?"

"That's easy. Get high. After tonight, I need it."

"Right," she says. "As someone who's been in your shoes before, I thought you would say that. Here, this might help." She points to the glove compartment. "Open it up. There's some cigarettes inside. Smoke those if you need to. But you're coming with me tonight. I'm not going to let you go home and destroy yourself."

She sounds like Eliza. No wonder they're friends. But I don't question her. Instead, I follow her directions and find the cheap cigarettes in the glove box. Never opened, a lighter attached with a rubber band. Moments later, and I'm on my second, then third cigarette. It does help.

"Better?"

"Yes, but why do you have them there?"

"In case I needed them. That pack has been there for over a year. They're probably no good. A fact that I'm very proud of."

No good for the average person, but anything right now is good enough for me. I'm ready for my fourth.

We pull into a cookie-cutter neighborhood on the east side of town where every house looks the same. Jessica hated houses like this, which is why we bought a historic home in the middle of the city—a house that has been habitually trashed for half a year.

"This is my house." She pulls into the drive and parks. "This is not normal for me. I do like to help people, but that doesn't usually involve bringing single men into my home."

"Montica might get jealous."

Her eyes turn angry. "Don't mock her. She's a good person and you better not ruin her."

I raise my hands in surrender.

Tessa exhales. "After a night like this, I could really use one of those cigarettes."

I hold the box out to her.

"No, I can't. And some day, I hope you can say the same thing."

I think of Pete, and how I don't want to turn into him. "Me too."

"There's a couch with your name on it. And no sneaking off and getting high. And you will spend the day with me tomorrow."

I pull out another cigarette and smile. "Don't you listen, babe? I've told you before, I'm not in to older women."

"Good. I'm not in to crackheads."

We laugh and then I sigh, if only to show her that I don't completely approve of her demands. But at this point, I'd rather give in then have to walk an hour home. And I owe her something for tonight. I'm not sure how I'll feel once the withdrawals start tomorrow, but I'll give her my best try.

"Okay, I guess I can give older women a try just this once."

She smiles. It's a beautiful smile. She's a beautiful woman. I've not given her enough credit before. "Well, I guess I can babysit if I have to. Follow me."

Chapter Eleven
Revelations

"Our dreams may dare reveal what our heart truly desires."

~Edward McClage

I dreamt of you last night. You were lying next to me and there were tears in your eyes. They were happy tears. Tears of joy, a welcome sight amidst the seemingly constant tears of sorrow we'd been used to.

I couldn't help but smile, because I knew our life was going to change forever. This was going to make things better for us. This is what we needed to get back on track, to feel again the love that brought us together.

You were beautiful. Like you always were before, but this time I could see the glow that I'd forgotten.

My arms could not embrace you enough. My lips could not kiss you enough. My heart could not love you enough. It was the perfect moment. My Jessica. My love.

The moment is shattered by the morning sun.

I try to keep my eyes closed, to bring myself back to that time, that place. It's impossible. I'll never be able to find that place again. I may see flashes, feel pieces of it, but I can't have it back. *Why God? Just one miracle. Take me back one more time.*

"Dude, you're finally awake."

The voice is unfamiliar. Young and filled with angst. I turn over on the small sofa as my eyes adjust to the room.

"You better hurry up and get ready."

The girl sits on a brown sofa, her legs dangling just short of the floor. "Hi," I manage.

"Hi to you too," she says, one eyebrow raised. "What sort of trouble landed you here with us?"

I shake my head, the throbbing of a migraine already present. I need something to take the edge off. "Who is *us*?"

"My mom and I," she answers.

I don't immediately make the connection, but then I note the resemblance, the long, black hair and the green eyes. "How old are you?"

She seems taken aback by my question. It's funny, because I asked her mom the same thing when I met her.

"I'm fourteen," she answers. "Why?"

Tessa said she was thirty years old. She would have had to have been sixteen when she had her. Was teen pregnancy part of Tessa's dark past?

"What's your name?"

"I'm Kalen." She slides forward. "Wait, you're not some type of like—pervert—or something."

I've been called many things, but never that. I laugh, while sitting up. "No, I'm not a very good person, but not that."

She grins, then stands up. "Yeah, I knew you had something wrong with you. Mom's always helping someone. That's her one fault."

I take in the small figure in front of me. She's wearing head to toe black, with a hint of red in the skirt. On her wrists are black straps with metal studs. The word rebellion comes to mind, and yet her demeanor says something different.

"I see you've found our guest," Tessa says, walking swiftly into the room. "I'm sorry if she's pestering you." Tessa adjusts the sleeves of her green dress. She has her hair pulled back into a bun with some type of ribbon wrapped in it.

"You bring home a stranger and I'm getting the questions?" Kalen quips. "Typical."

"I'm not a stranger," I say. "We're friends."

"That better be all," Kalen says, glaring at me. The look loses its edge after a second. She quickly retreats to the right side of the room and down a paneled hall.

Tessa points toward a plate of eggs and toast on the side table next to the couch. "Breakfast is served. Eat quickly so we can go. You promised the day, remember?"

I do remember, and now I'm regretting it. Every part of me wants to ask about her daughter. About her past. But I settle for the obvious question. "Okay, what does spending the day with you entail?"

Tessa stops in the middle of the room. "It's Sunday, silly, so of course, church."

I want to laugh, but all I can muster is a muted groan.

***

The smell of perfume lingered in the air, masking the odor of industrial cleaner. The bitter scent stung my nose. Seven months had passed since I'd been to church, but nothing had changed. Tessa sat down in the third row of pews, her skirt rising to sit just past her knee. My gaze shifted to the familiar pulpit.

The last place in the world.

I repeat.

The last place in the world I want to spend my day is in a church. God truly must have a sense of humor. After all, this was not just any church, but the one that Jessica and I used to attend. Eliza and Roman were there, along with many of our old friends. Once upon a time, dinner with the Pearsons was normal—Mr. Pearson told stories of war while Mrs. Pearson cleaned our house once a week. Then there was Pastor Greene, he introduced me to God, he even met me at work once and confronted me about missing church. I never missed another Sunday after that until I fell off the wagon. My entire former life was right here in this room, except for my art, of course.

No wait, I helped paint the cross scene in the children's room.

I bit my lip until it bled to cope with the scene around me. That, and the cigarettes before and after the service, pulled me through. Many people greeted me, shook my hand, asked about my life… more condolences. My family was wise enough to just smile and say hello. No questions, no invites for lunch. Just a wave or a nod. That's a miracle for my brother. I put on my best face, but practically sprinted out of the building as soon as it was over.

And that's all I'm saying about that religious dump. A belief in a sovereign God led me to this catastrophe of a life. I'll never go back to that blind faith. That ignorance.

Now, I find myself sitting in a swing beside Tessa. It's the same swing set we sat on three weeks ago, when she bribed me for company with my brother's money.

"You did great today."

"That was the worst two hours of my life since, well, you know."

"She was the love of your life, wasn't she? Your soul mate, if you will."

I stand up. Conversations like this break my heart over and over again. I feel sick to my stomach immediately. That's the last thing I need with the pounding headache I have. I pull out a cigarette and light up.

"It's okay if you don't want to talk about it," Tessa says, a very convincing level of concern in her voice. *Mom's always trying to help someone.* That's what Kalen had said.

"I don't want to talk about it. Let's talk about you for a change. Why didn't you tell me you had a daughter?"

"You didn't ask," she answers, a smirk on her face. She puts her hands on her dress to keep the wind from blowing it up.

"Was she an accident or a consequence of someone else's deviance?"

Her expression immediately turns serious. "The latter. She was certainly not a mistake or accident."

"Who was it?"

Tessa doesn't respond immediately. After a few short breaths, she answers. "My uncle. He raped me from the time I was twelve until I was fifteen. I was too afraid of him to tell anybody, so I carried it all—the guilt, the shame, and the agony for three years. It wasn't until I got pregnant that the truth came out."

Her story is more horrifying than I imagined. As self-absorbed as I am right now by my own withdrawal, my sympathy is almost surface level.

"He's in jail for life now. My parents—" she pauses and brushes her hand across her face. She's facing away from me, but I know she's wiping away tears. "My parents wanted me to give her up for adoption. I refused. As painful as it was to think that my child would forever remind me of my nightly torture, I couldn't let her go."

"My parents would hear nothing of it. They arranged for a local family who was childless to take her. They're rich and very, let's say, influential back home. The very idea that people might whisper how their grandchild was also their niece horrified them. They cared about their reputation more than they cared about us. So, I ran. I've not seen them since."

"Does Kalen know any of this?"

"All of it," Tessa says, turning back toward me. Her eyes are red and wet. "I told her a year ago."

I put my hand behind my neck and squeeze at the tension. "Why did Roman and Eliza want you to meet me? It sounds like you had a rough life, but I'm a drug addict.

We're not quite the same, my torture is self-inflicted, so unlike yours. How did they think you could help me?"

Tessa smiles again. "Well, my story doesn't end with running away. I had my child, but no one to guide me. When I didn't know what to do, I turned to the only thing I'd ever known. I sold my body for money. It's amazing how many perverts will pay for a young girl. There's a whole world of filth that most people don't even know about. And when that wasn't enough, I started selling drugs.

"Honestly, I did pretty well for myself and Kalen. I got us both out of a shelter by the time I was nineteen. Bought my first home by the time I was twenty-one."

I could see where the story was going. "You didn't just sell drugs, did you?"

"Of course not. I was a user. But it all led to this. That's why I said Kalen wasn't an accident."

I laugh inside. "Let me guess, God did all of this for a reason."

She nods.

"Bull crap."

"Yeah, it is bull crap." Tessa stands up. "I went to jail. I lost custody of Kalen. I almost threw away everything in order to stay high. By the time Kalen was six years old, she had been placed in three foster homes. I'd been to rehab twice and was told by a judge that I was one strike away from never seeing her again. So yeah, I do think it is bull crap. I don't deserve the life I have right now. Yet, apparently God thinks I do."

It's a cop-out answer. But I don't press any further. Instead, I retreat back to my swing. "Well, I'm glad everything worked out for you. Maybe someday I'll feel what you are feeling now, but at the moment, I just don't see God's *ever so* gracious plan."

Tessa reaches over and puts her hand on my arm. "I believe you will."

I shrug it away. "That's the winner in you talking. Easy for you to say now, you won your battle. I'm not where you are now. I'm still fighting my demons."

"I lost my child for two years. I lost my family. Can you imagine how hard that is?"

Her words strike a chord in my heart. "I lost it all too." I whisper the words without even thinking.

Tessa places her hand back on my arm. "I'm sorry. That came out wrong. I know—"

I stand again. "You're a strong woman, Tessa. It's no wonder Roman and Eliza came to you. I appreciate everything you've done for me, but I'm not worthy or ready for the savior routine. Let's go back to you being boss lady, and I'll go back to drug addicted has-been artist temporarily out of retirement."

I start to walk away, when for the third time, I feel her hand on my arm. This time, she holds on. I turn and face her.

"We can't go back. You see, I've shared my whole life with you, and you haven't shared very much with me at all. That's not fair. But even if you don't share anything else, I feel like I've been placed in your life for a reason, and I can't let that go."

I shake my head, just to show that I'm annoyed. "You're turning Joseph on me. The old man never lets things go."

"It's because we see something in you. You know why it was so hard for everyone to find you last night?"

Last night feels like an eternity ago. Seeing my parents seems like a dream. For a second, I wonder if my mother is back home trying to get herself killed again. "Because I have no friends."

Tessa smiles. "Well, there is that. But it's because the Art Studio was the last place anyone thought you'd be."

It's the last place I thought I'd be too. I can thank Ritchie for that inspiration. My thoughts turn toward that unfinished piece on my desk. *I want to finish it.*

"Okay, so I'm changing a little," I concede.

Tessa lets go of my arm. "That's progress."

I turn away. "Whatever you say, 'one night in London.' I think our day is over. I'll see you bright and early tomorrow morning."

"I sure hope so." Even with her unwavering optimism, I can tell she's hesitant to believe me.

Chapter Twelve
Picasso Has Nothing on You

Contrary to Tessa's belief, I'm up early today. I rise before dawn and step out beneath a moonless sky. Normally, I would just be going to bed after a binge, but the inspiration is bubbling, despite the pounding in my head. Lafayette has yet to wake and I walk along Ferry Street, past the cafe and the museum and, eventually, my sister-in-law's antique store, through pale pools of light cast by the street lamps. I begin hammering on the metal just after sunrise. I'm a little hungover, but three cups of coffee and several ibuprofens have kicked in, and I'm working up a sweat.

I'm hanging another iron bar and can't quite get one end to reach the bracket secured in the brick when Ritchie's hands suddenly appear under the metal. My assistant has saved the day, or at least my burning muscles.

We're sitting on the sidewalk sharing that third round of gas station coffee when the rest of the center's inhabitants show up. Tessa waves and I give her a nod and a smirk, as I'm sure she can see the progress already made this morning. She doesn't give me the satisfaction of a response.

Montica arrives last, a notebook in her hand, a smile on her face. She kisses me on the cheek. "How was your weekend?"

"Interesting," I answer, before kissing her mouth.

Ritchie rolls his eyes behind her.

Now, we find ourselves at a crossroads. I wave Ritchie to follow me. He's covered in sweat, but hasn't complained once. He grins, relishing any attention I give to him. Once we reach the street, I turn around and point toward the wall. "What do you see?"

Ritchie looks at me with an expression that denotes confusion.

"Just look at it. What do you see Ritchie?"

"Uhhmm… " he hesitates. "A w-wall."

I laugh, his answer providing me with the type of humor that's needed on a hot July day like this. The type of humor that takes my mind off of my cravings. "I see that, too. But, I'm talking about the project. The artwork."

As of now, we have seventeen iron bars bracketed in. The design is suspect at best, and to me resembles some type of maze. For some reason, Ritchie's inspiration did not carry through the weekend. Back when art was my life, I'd do this very thing. Step back and see what was forming. In fact, I'd done this very thing two nights ago in my old office. I'd seen something in those bars and barbed wire fence. In fact, I could still see that project in my mind. But this project—the one I'm being paid fifty thousand dollars in future drug money—eludes me.

"I d-don't know," Ritchie responds after a few moments. "It looks l-like a b-b-ball of y-yarn to me." His face turns red in embarrassment.

I place my hand on his shoulder, the first endearing thing I've done for my Down's part—no, *just my partner*. My mind won't let me categorize him anymore, not after what I saw on stage Saturday night. It's still hard for me to believe that he's some sort of guitar hero.

I tilt my head, if only to be dramatic. "I can see that too. But that's not what I'm asking either. What do you see it becoming from here? I can't see where it's going. But I think you can. So, what do you see? Or better yet, what do you think Roger would see?" Frankly, I don't care about this Roger, but I've got to find something to get this moving in the right direction. My first check won't last long if I'm buying hits nightly.

Ritchie smiles, baring his crooked teeth. He turns back toward the project and stares at it intently.

"What are you two doing?" Montica asks, stepping into the lawn. I can imagine we look like fools, my head tilted, Ritchie leaning over, as if having his eyes slightly closer to the work will help him decipher its future.

Montica bears a sheen of sweat, which glistens on her dark skin. She's allowing her hair to grow out, and for some reason, the darkness that's covering her once-shaved head just makes her even more beautiful.

"Seriously, what are you doing?"

I hold out my hand. "Shhh. This is important."

She starts to say something, but I place my hand over her mouth. I can feel her lips purse into a grin. She grabs my wrist and pulls my hand down. "Solving the world's problems, I see."

"S-something l-l-like that," Ritchie says, still staring at the wall.

I can't help but laugh. It feels good to laugh uninhibited. It's been a long time since I've done so. I stop it as soon as I'm able. I'm not allowed to feel that.

Montica shakes her head, then patiently waits.

Five minutes pass before Ritchie takes a step forward and nearly falls, his trance broken. I hold onto his shoulder. "I g-got it!" he yells.

"What?" Montica asks.

I make sure Ritchie is stable, before smartly answering. "A solution to the world's problems I presume."

She rolls her eyes.

"Tell me, what do you see for this project?"

Ritchie's eyes are wide with excitement. "W-well, Roger w-would have s-s-seen a c-circle too. B-but not y-yarn."

"Yarn?" Montica asks.

I cover her mouth again.

"N-no, it's the w-world."

I don't see his vision, but I let him continue.

"Roger w-wanted everyone t-to g-get along. The whole w-world. He was n-n-nice t-to... uh... everyone." Ritchie looks at me with anticipation.

I look at the current ball of yarn made out of metal pipes, then back to Ritchie. "That's really what you see?" I still see nothing, but my lack of inspiration affords me no real argument. At least we have a direction, which means the money will come sooner.

He nods.

I turn to Montica. "Then it looks like we are creating the world, planet Earth, on your wall."

She, too, looks at the mess of iron bars. "Really?"

"That's what the boy says Roger would want, so that's what Roger is going to get." I place my arm around Ritchie. "Good call." I guess.

He's too embarrassed to respond.

"Montica, write down the following items in that little notebook of yours." My mind is racing with material ideas, some far-fetched and ridiculous, others much more practical, but far less amusing. Really, none of them make sense, but that's just how it works. Now that we have some direction, I'm confident that I can get this done soon.

After wearing out her writing hand, I pause. "Sound good, Ritchie?"

He nods, still smiling from ear to ear.

"That's good," Montica says, closing the notebook. "Because this is going to cost more than we are paying you."

I shrug my shoulders. "I'm sure generous donors will agree. You could always ask Bob for the money."

She rolls her eyes a second time. "We'll see. On that note, we should probably call it a day. Your Picasso will have to wait until I get the material."

The mess of iron bars and brackets doesn't lend itself to the famous painter's work, but I know what she's getting at. It's the strangeness of it, the angles, the abstractness that lends the comparison.

Ritchie slides away from my grasp. "P-picasso h-has nothing on y-you," he says. "I'll see y-you t-t-tomorrow."

"He's right," she says.

"Yeah, we'll see about that when this project is over." I start back toward the building. She follows me.

I start to pick some of the materials up, but stop when I notice she's standing expectantly beside me. I hesitantly give her my attention.

She bites her lip before talking. "Thanks for leaving a note the other night. From what I hear, most men aren't that thoughtful."

She's holding on to that dream still, the one where I clean up my act and we live happily ever after.

I start to work again, but she doesn't move. After stacking a couple of bars, I turn toward her. "Tomorrow night. Seven?"

She grins. "It's a date."

Ritchie appears beside me as she wanders away. "I f-forgot my l-l-unchbox." When he bends to pick up the cooler, his shirt lifts ever so slightly revealing a nasty gap of black and purple welts. The bruise covers the width of his back, and who knows how high or low it goes. It's a terrible wound, and I wince, immediately picturing Pete's wife, the bruises that he no doubt leaves on her. Is Ritchie being abused?

"S-see y-you tomorrow," Ritchie says, passing me. I'm bent over, frozen in place, and probably look like an idiot.

There's a sudden surge of anger inside of me. I'm not sure where this sudden protective feeling is coming from. Why should I care? And more importantly, what can I do?

Chapter Thirteen
The Abused

It's seven in the morning and I already hear screaming from inside the dilapidated house as I near the front lawn. A man's voice. The smoke swirls around me in the early morning air as I chain smoke another half pack of cigarettes.

It wasn't hard to find. Ritchie told me his small yellow house was two blocks from the resource center, and there it is. The only yellow structure on this stretch of 30th street—a one-story, run-down building with old wooden siding. The yellow paint is chipping away, and I can see piles of it in the corners between the walls and cement porch. Large bushes conceal much of the front, and vines grow up the sides of the chimney. If it were brick, it would be the prime subject for ghost stories.

I stub out another butt and chuck it aside. I smoked at least three dozen cigarettes last night while pacing my house over and over. I couldn't get that bruise out of my mind. I wanted to, I contemplated buying enough drugs to force the forgetful fog, but my conscience, that little part of me that seems to be coming alive again, wouldn't let me. My blood boils just listening to the shouting, in fact, it's been boiling ever since I saw the marks yesterday.

This wouldn't have been an issue three days ago. I wouldn't have cared. But that date with Montica, Ritchie's guitar playing, and my late-night art project did something to me. Some part of me now cares, it's a very small part of me, but it's there nonetheless. It'd be so much easier if it weren't.

Sleep finally came, but only after I'd made the decision to look into things myself. And so, here I am.

"I don't care!" the voice yells.

I hide behind a tree as the front door opens. Ritchie stumbles out, his mouth in a forced frown. He takes a few steps and then turns around. "I f-forgot my l-lunch inside."

I can see the figure inside the doorframe, but beyond that, it's dark. "I said I don't care!" he yells.

"B-b-but I n-n-n-need it," Ritchie says, his stuttering more apparent with the addition of tears.

He's never said anything about his family. Ritchie's a talented and smart kid, and so I assumed he had the independence to live on his own. He is an adult.

Why am I here? I'm not sure if I'll be able to answer that question. I really don't have time to.

I see the fist connect with Ritchie's chest before my mind can even process it. My friend stumbles backward a few steps, but stands his ground. Ritchie is strong. "I'm g-getting it," he says.

The man laughs. "Do you like getting hurt? Your mom sure did. Right up until she bit the bullet." He hits Ritchie again.

I step out from behind the tree. "C'mon Ritchie, I'll buy you lunch."

Ritchie turns and quickly wipes the tears from his eyes.

I can see the man clearly now, short like Ritchie, but with long hair. He's stocky, his arms probably the size of Roman's, but much less muscular. Certainly large enough to inflict pain. He steps out of the doorway and onto the porch, wearing only sweat pants, his large gut hanging over the waistband.

Why would Ritchie still live here? He has so much going for him.

I expect the man to say something, but he just grins. With one hand, he grabs Ritchie's shoulder and pushes him out toward me. I have every intention of hurling curses and threats at the vile man, but he just turns and walks inside. The door is closed before I can even form one word.

"W-why are you here?" Ritchie asks, his head facing the ground.

I put my arm around his shoulders. "I saw the bruise on your back yesterday."

Ritchie shrugs my arm off, then starts down the road. I follow him, but don't say anything. When we reach the end of the block, he turns toward me, clearly upset. "I n-n-n-ever asked y-y-you to h-help me," he says.

I give him my best smile. "I couldn't let it go."

"You should," he responds, before turning and walking down the adjacent street.

I continue to walk behind him wordlessly, trying to process how such a talented young man would stay in an abusive atmosphere, and how the staff at the Resource Center would let this go on. Surely, they know. Just seeing the condition of his home life is warrant for a drink. I can't imagine being abused. Sure, I've done a lot to myself, but that's different.

It's not until the center is in sight that I approach the subject again. "Ritchie, can we just talk about this?"

He stops in the middle of the road and sighs. "I'll t-t-talk after music. C-come to m-my b-b-band practice tonight."

I step in front of him and put my hand out. "Is that an official invitation into the cool crowd?"

He does his best not to smile, but he can't hide the thin line that forms between his lips. "S-sure." He shakes my hand.

***

Tessa is clad in sweatpants and a black tank top when she swings open her front door—not her usual well-kept appearance—and I'm taken aback. In fairness, she looks just as surprised to see me at her door.

"You weren't at the center today."

Tessa just nods and reluctantly lets me in.

It's Kalen who invites me to stay for dinner, albeit in a very antagonistic tone, which garners a very pointed glance from her mother. Of course, I oblige.

But not once has Tessa asked me why I'm here. Kalen doesn't say much either. I realize that having some messed up stranger in their house isn't all that abnormal. Kalen said as much the morning I met her. *Mom's always trying to help someone.*

I finish my portion of meat casserole first, then study the pair in front of me. If not by age, and the liberal use of black—clothes, eyeliner, fingernails—on Kalen, they could be twins. It's interesting and scary at the same time.

Tessa catches me staring and clears her throat. "How was your day?"

"Fine. Yours? Where were you by the way?"

She smiles, but it's a tired gesture. "It was fine. I had an appointment elsewhere."

I see Kalen bite her lip, but she continues to eat.

Ignoring the obvious signs between the two, I state my purpose for the visit. "Why is Ritchie being abused and why is no one doing anything about it?"

Tessa appears to wake up immediately. She turns to Kalen. "Can you excuse us?"

Kalen puts down her fork. "Looks like you struck a nerve," she says to me. "I'll eat in the living room." She grabs her plate and retreats from the kitchen.

Tessa waits a few seconds, her expression now stern. She moves her chair closer to mine and leans forward, nearly whispering. "How did you find out?"

I lean toward her in a mocking gesture and whisper. "I'm not blind."

Returning to her normal seated position, she sighs. "No, you're not. But that is confidential information. I can't give out Ritchie's info to just anybody."

"I'm not anybody."

"Yes, you are. All I can say is that we've tried to get him to move. He's an emancipated adult. But it's his uncle, and Ritchie refuses to leave. He's had scholarship offers to several colleges, and he's refused. His uncle is all the family he has left. APS and the police have been involved in the past, but the system has failed." Tessa scoots her chair back, a sign that she's done with this conversation.

I'm not. "I can do something."

"No, you can't."

"I know people."

"I'm sure you do, but don't stick your nose where it doesn't belong." Tessa reaches out and grabs my hand. "Please, just let it go."

I pull away immediately, a plan formulating in my mind. It's a bad idea, but I don't care. I'm not sure why Ritchie's safety has become so important to me. I'm not sure why I've allowed the boy into my life at all. Anyone for that matter. Why am I stringing Montica along? Why am I here with Tessa now? I should be home, killing myself.

"Let me ask you this. Would his uncle be interested in money?"

Tessa gives me a suspicious look. "Why?"

"Well, I think I can finish the project in a few weeks and then I'll get paid. I have enough money to buy drugs for some time, and I can spare some change."

Her expression changes from suspicion to surprise. She smiles. "Wait, you want to go out of your way to help someone? Are you okay?"

I don't feel like I know her well enough to take such an offensive question. Too bad she's right. I don't believe it either. But that's enough. I stand, pushing my chair from the table. "I'll take that as a yes. The money will do."

She stands too. "Where are you going?" She follows me to the front door. Kalen gives me a half-hearted wave from the couch. I turn when I feel Tessa's hand on my arm again. "Tell me, what are you going to do?"

I grin. "Nothing yet. I've got a band practice to attend."

Chapter Fourteen
Animal Instinct

I lied to Tessa. I didn't go to Ritchie's band practice. Instead, I found Pete. Pete has a gun. Pete is intimidating. Pete is a cheap option.

After leaving a message with Montica, letting her know that I wouldn't be stopping by tonight, I hopped in to Pete's Trailblazer. He inspects his gun, then places it in the back of his pants, before covering the black metal with his shirt. "So, why are we doing this again? What does this boy mean to you?"

"Don't worry about it. I paid you, and that should be enough."

Pete wipes his nose with his sleeve and starts the SUV. "Whatever. I just thought since I'm risking years in jail for you, I could at least get some answers. But money is money." Pete's concerned I'm changing, that I'm not actually just like him.

I don't respond. This is probably the worst thing I've done to this point.

Pete speeds through town, and we're in front of Ritchie's house in about five minutes. It's just about dark, and I hope that Ritchie's practice is longer than a couple of hours. I'm not sure what I'll do if Ritchie is home.

My phone buzzes. Two missed calls from Tessa. The newest buzz a text from Joseph. She must have called him. They suspect I'm crazy enough to do something like this. They suspect right. I place the phone back into my pocket.

"Are you sure about this?" Pete asks.

"Why? Are you afraid?"

Pete fakes a laugh. The pupils of his eyes are so large, they remind me of marbles. "This is just another day for me." He turns the Blazer off and gets out.

"Let's just do this quickly."

Pete bows and points to the porch. "After you, fearless leader."

My heart's beating out of my chest, but I force myself to approach the front door. The rotten steps squeak under my feet, causing my body to tremble, nerves rattling. Before I allow myself the opportunity to forget that any of this happened, and run away, I'm knocking on the door. I don't turn around, but I can feel Pete's presence behind me.

We wait a few seconds, although it feels like an eternity. *Maybe he's not home.* I'm beginning to hope so, but then I hear the telltale sound of the door handle turning.

I don't even have time to react. I see the man's face, horror written all over it. Pete is in front of me, the gun pointed at the man's face. Pete grabs the fat man by his tattered shirt and pushes him inside as if he's done this a million times. He probably has.

I feel numb. He's done this to me. I know how this man must feel right now. I shake the thought away and force myself inside.

"Get down on your knees!" Pete yells.

Ritchie's uncle is sobbing as he lowers himself onto the stained carpet. The house is dark and disgusting, trash everywhere—it's just filthy. It looks like my house, except this one has had years of mistreatment.

"Don't kill me!" the man pleads.

"What's your name?" Pete asks, pushing the gun into the crying man's forehead.

"Bill," he mutters. "Please, please don't kill me. I'll do whatever you want."

There's hardly any furniture in the house, but there's a mattress in the middle of the main living area. I'm pretty sure I see cockroaches walking across it, which makes my stomach churn. I can't imagine Ritchie living in this dump. The boy who has so much potential, stuck in a place like this. I'm convinced that even if everything about this is wrong, it's worth the risk to help him. I can't let him do this to himself. I can't let him be like me, forcing himself into a life that is a waste.

I'm drawn out of my thoughts by a loud crack, followed by Bill's sobbing. I turn just in time to see the man double over, clenching his face.

"I think I broke his nose," Pete says maniacally.

The realization that the cracking noise was Bill's nose makes my stomach churn even more. I'm trying to save Ritchie, not become more like Pete. Sure, it's for someone else, but to threaten a man's life goes far beyond threatening my own with drugs and alcohol. I'm practically vibrating with nerves and energy. I shift my stance for the umpteenth time. I'm not sure Jessica would even recognize the man I am right now—a strung out junkie committing a home invasion and an assault.

So, I quickly step between the two before Pete does any more damage.

I see the blood seeping through Bill's fingers. He looks up toward me, his eyes pleading for mercy. I know he recognizes me from this morning.

"Let me hit him again," Pete says. "He'll be a little more understanding then."

I raise my hand to let Pete know that I've got it. Then, I kneel beside the bloody, tearful mass. "Listen to me." I grab his collar to pull him closer.

"I'm sorry. I'm so sorry," he wails. "I won't hit the boy again. I promise."

"I know," I respond. "There's only one thing you'll do. When he gets home tonight, you're going to tell him that he is going to college to pursue his music career. Don't worry about the money. I'll make sure he gets it. Then, we are going to help him make that dream come true. You will do nothing but provide a place for him to stay. That's it. Okay?"

Bill nods vehemently.

"Good. If you don't do what I say, my friend here will be visiting again soon, and he won't hesitate to kill you. Understood?"

"Yes, anything you say."

I throw him back to the ground. "We have a deal then." I reach into my pocket and pull out a stack of one hundred-dollar bills, then scatter them over his slumped figure. "Here's two thousand dollars for your troubles. If you do everything I say, I'll give you another thousand in a month." I'm lying. This will be enough. I know he won't come after any more money. "And clean this place up. You're disgusting."

It hurts a little throwing the money away. I'm running low on my original payment, but I know I'm only a few weeks from finishing the art project, and there will be plenty more where that came from. In the end, giving the man some money is the least I can do for allowing Pete to put a gun to his face and break his nose.

"I hope you screw up," Pete yells over my shoulder.

I push him away. "Let's go." We've done what we came here to do. And I don't need another strike on my police record. I certainly don't want to be caught doing anything with Pete again. We're both strung out on coke, but he's on strike two hundred and is probably wielding his gun illegally.

Pete spits over my shoulder, but complies.

The outside air hits my face and feels like freedom. I take a deep breath, still holding onto Pete. He struggles to put his gun away, but still has the wherewithal to allow himself a giddy laugh, as if he'd just beaten up a kid in the schoolyard. I realize Pete was the perfect person for the job, but I'm a little afraid that I gave meat to a wild animal.

"You could have done without the money. The man nearly pissed himself."

Once we reach the SUV, I let go of Pete's arm. "I wouldn't have been able to live with myself."

Pete laughs even harder. "You still trying to change? How many times do I have to tell you that you're just like me? You can't change, man." He turns the key and the old vehicle roars to life.

Although I do feel just like him, I know that I'm more. I feel it. But there's no real use in trying to convince him otherwise.

"Your silence tells me you agree."

"Just go."

He puts the Blazer into gear. "As you wish, partner."

As we speed away, I see Ritchie through the rear-view mirror, his guitar slung over his shoulder. Although he'd never recognize Pete's car, I still duck away. When we are a safe distance, I look in the mirror again, just in time to see Ritchie walk into his yard.

I can't help but smile. I broke my promise. I missed his band practice. But, if Bill follows through, Ritchie won't care about that soon. This should be the beginning of a new life for him.

Chapter Fifteen
Results

"No amount of sin will win you a war."

~Edward McClage

Time is like me today, trying to get upstairs after a Friday night bender—it's crawling. I glance at the door and hold my breath. I'm the picture of paranoia and I know it. Every five minutes, I check the window outside my house, as if there are police cars lining the curb. I can imagine Ritchie's uncle screaming and cursing, his face bruised and broken.

Pete and I smoked and drank for several hours last night. In fact, Pete is still on my floor, I kick him as I walk by to make sure he's still alive.

My walk to the center seems like a blur, and as I round the corner of Cason and 27th, I have this nagging feeling that it is going to turn into a long day.

Fortunately, there are no crowds, no police cars, and no bruised and broken Bill. The small lawn in front of the A.W.A Resource Center is quiet, save a couple of staff walking toward the front door with a group of clients.

It's too quiet.

It's not until I reach the parking lot that I see Joseph's car. And beside it, a familiar Jeep. Bob's jeep. *What am I walking into?*

I'm barely in the lot when Tessa walks out of the building. "I need you to come with me now," she says.

"Sorry, I missed your calls."

"Come on," she repeats sternly. She's already back in the building before I can say more.

I smoke a cigarette before gathering the nerve to walk inside. In the main lobby, I search the staff for Montica. She's nowhere to be found.

"They're in the conference room," the woman at the front desk says. "Straight through that door there."

"Thanks," I reply, then find myself face to face with the young girl who only says "hi." *Angela.*

"Hi," she says three times in succession.

I nod.

"Hi," she responds again.

"There you are, Angela," one of the staff women says, walking through another door. She's young and doesn't look familiar. She must be new. "I've been looking all over for you."

"Hi," Angela responds as the staff takes her hand and guides her toward the front office.

I say "hi" in a whisper, but Angela is already gone. I take a deep breath before walking through the door I was pointed toward. It leads me down a narrow hallway on the other side, and I can immediately see the conference room where big fat Bob looks angry. I want to slide back through the door, but his beady eyes latch on to me.

"It's about time!" he hollers.

Tessa appears in the doorway. "Come in."

Joseph is sitting on the other side of the table. All three sets of eyes seem to bore into me. Only Joseph offers a quick smile.

"I'm sure you know why you are here," Tessa says, before sitting down.

"Where's Montica?" I ask, ignoring the initial question.

"She called in sick," Tessa answers. There's a sternness in her voice that I have only seen once, when I had asked for my check two weeks ago. The way her eyes narrow and her jaw clenches brings out some sort of wild beauty. She may be several years older than me, but she's growing on me in some way. I'm not sure if I can explain it. I guess it's always the same thing. She reminds me of Jessica. That's definitely what it is.

"Why don't you have a seat," Joseph says.

"Please do," Bob adds, clearly agitated.

I comply. "What's wrong, Bob? Did your breakfast get interrupted this morning?"

"Why you—" Bob bites his tongue, but I know his mind is going through his list of curses. "You're getting paid a small fortune to do this project. The least you can do is try not to screw things up."

I raise my hands if only to be dramatic. "Why don't one of you tell me what's going on."

"As if you don't alrea—"

"I think you know exactly why we are all here," Tessa interrupts Bob, whose face is now beet red. "Ritchie came in today saying that Bill told him to go to college. That Bill's face looked beat up. And that Bill wanted him to pursue his music any way he could. He also said that the two of them spent hours cleaning the place yesterday. So, we want to know what you did."

I give my best innocent look. "I don't know what you're talking about."

"Don't lie!" Bob yells, beating his fat hand on the table.

"I'm not. I think it's great that this Bill guy wants Ritchie to go to school. I can't agree with him more. I think Ritchie deserves it. He's talented. If it wasn't for him, the project wouldn't be near the point it is now." I try to subtly alter my overly enthusiastic response toward the end.

Tessa closes the door, probably to conceal Bob's loud mouth.

Joseph places his hand on my arm. The old softy's eyes look watery already. "That's great to hear, but are you really telling us the truth? I know this doesn't really have much to do with us, but Tessa thought if you were doing some—well—shady business that it might affect the job, and that it might affect both the center and the Art Studio negatively."

I shake my head. "I don't know what you're talking about."

Bob looks like he is about to explode, but he doesn't say anything.

Joseph pulls his hand away. "Well, you heard the man. He doesn't know a thing."

I could be mistaken, but I think I see a slight grin on Tessa's face. If there is one, it vanishes quickly. "Great, glad that that's settled. Now let's get down to business. How are we going to help Ritchie get into school? We could barely calm him down today, he's so excited. I invited Bob and Joseph down here since they've worked closely with you for years. But, since you *didn't do anything,* I thought we could also get their input on some job ideas for Ritchie, since they are heavily involved in community affairs."

"And we appreciate you thinking of us," Joseph says. Bob doesn't appear near as appreciative. But that's just Bob. He's still eying me, hoping that I'll give something away I'm sure. He was probably in the middle of his morning bourbon when they called him.

"Unfortunately, I'm not sure how we can be of service," Bob mutters. "We have no job openings available at the Studio right now. We are a not-for-profit organization, so it's not like we can just create a job for the kid."

"He's an adult," Tessa fires back. She has the fire that Montica had when I first met her. Bob seems to bring that out in people.

"You can't come up with anything?" I ask. "Come on, Bob. With all that money I'm making you right now?"

Bob shakes his head, his double chin playing catch up. "Wes, you know, if you'd decide to come back and do some more work for us, instead of moping around for six months, maybe we'd have a little more money."

"Bob!" Joseph says sharply.

I should be upset at Bob's insensitive remark. How could he understand what it's like to lose a wife? All he lost was a receptionist and one of his prized artists. I know for a fact he had Jessica's position filled within a few days of her death.

But I'm not mad at him. I'm not sure why. "You're right, Bob, I should get back to work." The fat man's eyes grow wide, as if I'd given him a million dollars. Well, in a sense, if I did come back, that's exactly what I'd be doing. "But right now, let's focus on getting Ritchie some work."

Bob recovers. "Well, I just don't have anything. It's not a great market downtown right now. I don't know of anybody hiring."

The word *downtown* sticks in my mind. I know of someone downtown. I don't think of them often, and when I do, it's usually in a negative sense. But there's no one I know, besides Tessa, who likes to help people more. Annoyingly so.

"I have an idea."

They all look toward me.

"And?" Tessa asks.

"Well, it's a long shot, but I think I can work the system."

Tessa's eyes widen with knowledge, she's on to my plan.

"It'll take me cleaning up my act, but if I can help Ritchie, then I'll consider it worth it."

Bob's mouth is agape. Joseph gives me a grin as if every little bit of change he sees in me is worth the world.

"Do you think they'll do it?" Tessa asks.

"Well, my brother won't necessarily want to, but Eliza is a do-gooder. She can't pass up the idea of helping someone in need, and trust me, she's persistent. I don't know if they can offer much, but it's at least something."

Bob stands up. "Sounds like you have a plan. I'll be out of your way."

No one objects as the fat man departs.

"Sorry about Bob," Joseph says, an apologetic look on his wrinkled face.

"It's okay," Tessa responds. "Montica told me a little about him."

"He's a good man at heart."

"You're too nice," I say. "He's a pig and you know it."

Joseph doesn't immediately respond, so I take it he agrees with me. He'll never say it, but I know deep down inside Joseph resents Bob on many levels. He sighs, then speaks. "Eliza and your brother own the antique shop just down the road from the Art Studio, correct?"

I nod.

"Well, I leave it in your hands. It sounds like a good plan for the boy—I mean the young man." Joseph stands up from the table. "I'll take my leave as well." He gives me another grin as he walks by.

As soon as Joseph is out of the room, Tessa shakes her head, her lips in a thin line.

"What?"

She rolls her eyes. "I don't know what you did, but I'm sure it wasn't good. Ritchie's uncle is not a man to be trifled with."

"Well, he's letting Ritchie go to school, so he can't be that bad."

Tessa exhales loudly. "You're sticking to your story, huh?"

"Just telling you what I know."

"Whatever you say," she replies. "You better go get Ritchie. You'll probably never get more work out of him than you will today."

I stand up.

"You know, you really are changing."

I think of Pete beating Bill with the butt of his gun. Pete once said I was just like him. And some days I still am. But its days like today that show me that I can do more. That I can still do something good. A month ago, I would have laughed at the thought. That being said, I brought Pete with me. I threatened Ritchie's uncle. I got so high last night. I'm still in the pit.

I hear Ritchie's voice echo down the hall. "I'm g-going to s-s-chool!"

"And you once told me you wanted to die. I knew you didn't," Tessa says.

Tessa shifts in her seat, and for a split second, I see Jessica before me, her resoluteness visible in her blue eyes. I immediately want to embrace her, but then Tessa's green eyes and wide smile appear. I catch my breath, fall back into reality.

Chapter Sixteen
Sunday Dinner

"They're your family," she says. Jessica runs her fingers down my bare back, drawing some indeterminate design. "You can at least give them some of your time."

I roll over on the couch, placing my face directly below her chest. "There's only twenty-four hours in a day. If you haven't noticed, I'm a little busy most days."

She gives me a half smile. "No one should ever be too busy for their family. Not even if they are famous."

"You think I'm famous?" I quip.

She rolls her eyes, those beautiful blue circles that stole my heart. "I think you're good at ignoring my point. How can I expect you to want a family with me if you can't even make time for the family you have now?"

I start to speak, but no words form. There is nothing I can say that will combat her logic. She's right. I let out a noticeable sigh. "You win."

"I always do."

***

In the end, she lost. We both lost.

It's been five days since I last saw Montica. I spent the better half of yesterday leaving messages on her phone, none of which were returned. Since our first date, this is the longest I've gone without seeing her, and I have a suspicion that I'm being ignored. I can think of several reasons why a beautiful, smart woman like her would want to steer clear of my messy life, but none of my less-than-positive traits have ever pushed her away before.

But that's yesterday's news. Today is not about Montica or whatever it is that we have going on between is.

For that matter, it's not about me. That's a strange thought for me. *It's about someone else.*

Today, it's about Ritchie.

Before I can even step into his drive, I see Roman standing alert at his doorway, like a sentry. I cover my eyes, pretending his bright attire is hurting them. "Do you have something to wear that's not so prep school tennis player?"

He ignores my joke and wraps his hulking arms around me. "I can't believe you're actually doing something for someone else."

I force him off of me, just in time to see the glint in his eyes. "Come on, stop it. It's nothing."

"No, it's something," he responds. "And Mom and Dad called this morning before church. They said you visited yesterday. Mom repeated it three times before I believed her."

It's true, after calling Montica all morning and failing, I decided to keep the promise I'd made to my mother in the hospital. It cost me a fortune in cab fees, but I haven't seen my parents that happy since my wedding day. *I hate to say it, but I'm glad I saw them.*

"You're acting like Joseph, softy."

Roman puts his firm grip on my shoulder. "Well, stop with the heroics, and I'll stop being soft."

Heroics? Had he saw how Pete and I negotiated Ritchie's future a few days ago, he'd surely take back that statement. I'm far from good. The line of cocaine I did this morning is proof enough of that.

"Is Tessa here with Ritchie yet?"

Roman ushers me inside. "Not yet, but we left church before her. Speaking of Tessa, I hear you two are getting along well."

His question is leading, and as we enter his immaculate living room, I can see an almost giddy expression on his face. Apparently, even though Tessa is close with my brother and Eliza, she hasn't told them about my trysts with one of her staff members. I have to admit, Tessa is growing on me, even if she's hell-bent on cleaning me up. She's too much like Jessica, which is both endearing and painful.

Eliza enters the living room with the air of sophistication that always precedes her. "There's the runaway. You plan on staying a little longer this time?"

"I don't know, are—" My smart remark is interrupted by the doorbell.

Eliza scoots through the room, her professional attire unsettling. She seems much more at home than when she was stepping through the trash in my house.

Roman and I stare wordlessly at each other while we hear multiple greetings come from the foyer. I hear Ritchie's stuttering followed by a loud exclamation from Kalen. "Holy crap, this place is a mansion. Are we having tea with the queen?"

"Kalen!" Tessa says in a tone that I'm quite familiar with.

The group files into the living room, and Eliza is quick to give proper introductions. "This is my husband, Roman."

Roman stands up with an extended hand, and I imagine his grip crushing each hand he shakes.

"I-I'm Ritchie." My friend ignores Roman's hand and gives him a hug. The big softy embraces Ritchie like a long-lost friend. They were meant to work together. I hope.

"And this is Tessa's daughter, Kalen," Eliza says. "Of course, you know that since we go to church together."

"Yo," Kalen says with a single wave. "Nice crib. Mom's told me a lot about you both."

Roman's tennis attire and Kalen's black ensemble are quite the contrast.

"Hello." Roman then turns to Tessa and gives her one of those awkward formal hugs accompanied by a kiss on her cheek.

After the introductions are made, I stand up. "Hi."

Tessa takes a step toward me, then stops, clearly unsure how to greet me after such a formal display from Roman.

"Don't worry," I say, extending my hands. "I don't want to touch you either." Kalen and Ritchie laugh. Eliza gives me a pensive stare, but relaxes when Tessa smiles and rolls her eyes.

"Sorry we took so long. I got stuck at church a little longer than usual."

"Did Jesus have more work for you?" I ask. "Who wanted your help this time?"

Tessa ignores me and continues talking to Eliza. I don't mind. There's something about her dismissive expression that brings out her beauty. I force my mind to think of something else.

Kalen steps beside me. "This place really is cool."

"You should see the dungeon," I tell her.

"D-dungeon?" Ritchie questions, his eyes growing twice their normal size. Apparently, his unintended humor is funnier than my smart mouth, because everyone laughs.

I put my arm around his shoulder. "Yep, Roman keeps his bright wardrobe down there, away from the eyes of the general public."

Ritchie smirks.

"I'm about ready to take you down there," Roman adds dryly.

"Okay," Eliza announces, "let's talk more over lunch. Follow me."

We follow Eliza into the dining room and settle in.

After a moment, Kalen breaks the silence. "Do you seriously use all of this silverware at every meal?" Kalen holds up both forks and both knives.

"Seriously," I add, "but at least it gives us more options to jab in our eye when the dry topics ensue."

"Watch it," Eliza says.

Roman laughs. "When you run a successful business, you tend to mingle with other successful people, which means formal table settings and proper etiquette."

"You sound arrogant," I reply.

"And stuck up," Kalen adds.

"Kalen!" Tessa sternly says.

Laughter ensues.

I've got to give it to Roman, it takes a lot to offend my brother. Eliza not so much, and I can see the disdain in her eyes, but her look softens at everyone else's joy.

And that's how the dinner continues. I'm fairly certain that I haven't laughed this hard in years. Honestly, I don't remember the last time that I sincerely laughed. *What a terrible thought!* But between Ritchie's lack of etiquette, and Kalen's ignorance of a proper table setting, even Eliza can't help but succumb to the humor.

"You know, it's been a while since we've seen you so comfortable, Wes," Eliza says.

I stifle my laughter. I'm too comfortable. I don't like it. This isn't me. Another line would be perfect now. "Yeah, well, don't get used to it. Why don't we get down to business?"

Roman puts his napkin on the table and immediately goes into business mode. "So, Ritchie, you want a part-time job to help pay for school?"

Ritchie nods vigorously. "Y-yes, m-m-my uncle says I c-can g-g-go to school, b-but we d-don't have enough m-money."

I catch Tessa giving me a slight grin. For a moment, I see Jessica sitting across from me. I shake the image away to find Tessa's attention on Roman.

For the next few minutes, I find myself rotating glances between Tessa and Kalen, comparing the similarities between the two. Long black hair, dark green eyes, and fair skin. It's a little unsettling how similar they look, and my mind wanders to clones and government conspiracies. One thing I do know is that even if Kalen continues to embrace this dark, edgy gothic façade, she will eventually grow into the beautiful woman beside her.

Tessa now stares back at me, curiosity sparking in her eyes. Again, I can't help but displace her face with the image of my former wife. Jessica looks at me with a mix of attentiveness and concern, as if the entire world is resting in the thoughts that lie in my tiny brain.

I long for those eyes, the ones that usually came before a long embrace, maybe the throes of passion. I can almost feel her touching my skin, her smooth fingers caressing the side of my face.

There are things that I miss, and then there are things that I can't bear to think of missing—the warmth of her breath on my neck, watching her make coffee before work, listening to her hum her favorite song. Sometimes, I swear I can feel these things, I can see them, I can hear them. And that's what kills me inside. That's what kills me now.

That familiar pain in my chest returns, and the beautiful face of my wife is replaced with the face of another beautiful woman. She's not Jessica, and her eyes now have a narrowed focus in them. I turn away from Tessa's gaze, just as Roman turns over his company spiel to allow Eliza to talk about the day-to-day operations of their antique shop.

I take my brief lapse in reality as an indication that it's time for me to leave. I need a mask of some sort, whether that be a drink or a hit, just something to push these feelings back down.

I become the center of attention as I push my chair back from the table to stand. "I'm sorry, but it's time for me to jet." Eliza starts to speak, but I cut her off. "It's been wonderful. The food was great." She still has that look in her eyes that tells me she wants to counter my statement, so I lean over and kiss her on the cheek, not unlike what I used to do when Jessica and I came for our weekly Sunday lunch.

Eliza takes a deep breath.

"You have a glow," I tell her. As I pull away, I see her hand on her belly, as if my words remind her of the life growing inside. The words hurt more than I can express, but I needed to say them.

"Be good," Roman says, but doesn't try to stop me from leaving. I'm not sure if it's my sudden departure or soft gestures that are the most surprising, but I leave a room full of stunned faces.

Once I'm outside in the warm air, I take a deep breath. I feel tears forming. *This was supposed to be about Ritchie* I tell myself. *Get a hold of yourself.*

I barely take two steps when I hear the front door open. "Wait."

I turn toward Tessa. "Is this going to become a habit? You can't follow me every time I leave my brother's house. They're going to think something is going on?"

She grins, but it quickly disappears. "What was that back there?"

"I don't know. I guess I got a little sentimental or something. It's not every day that I'm nice to Eliza. You witnessed something miraculous. Lucky you."

Tessa walks down the steps. "No," she says, stopping just in front of me, "not that. You were staring at me for like five minutes. You looked like you were in some other world. I almost said something, but then you snapped out of it and excused yourself."

I shift away. "It's nothing. I just left reality for a moment."

Tessa grabs my arm. "Why do you continue to do that? You can talk to me. I'm listening."

Her words grip my heart and squeeze. Jessica gave me a variation of those very words so many times. She always listened to me, even if I didn't give her half the attention she deserved.

I turn toward Tessa, and I can't help but see Jessica again. It's like they were cut from the same mold, always trying to help, always trying to champion a cause. Beautiful and naïve.

Deep down, I know that she isn't Jessica, but the similarities pull me toward her. My lips meet hers, and for a moment, I hold her tight against me, kissing her unashamedly.

It's brief, and her hands soon push softly against my chest. "What are you doing?"

I shake my head, trying to understand it myself. It wasn't like kissing Montica, where only pleasure was involved. This kiss was different. "I'm sorry."

Tessa touches her mouth, but doesn't respond.

"I really am sorry." I don't feel sorry, but it's the right thing to say.

The door closes behind her, and Kalen leans against it. "I'm going to pretend that was a one-time affair."

Tessa moves toward her daughter. "Yes, it was. Let's go back inside."

Kalen smiles wryly at me as her mother pushes her back into the house. "See you around."

The door closes, and I'm left alone.

Chapter Seventeen
The Words of a Wise Man

If I were to compare Ritchie to an inanimate object today, it would be a rocket ship ready to blast off. Needless to say, he got the job. At least that's what he's told me a million times today, and although his enthusiasm is usually contagious, I can't help but feel an absence. Montica didn't come to work again. It's just not the same without her. The work is getting done, but without her here to share in our progress, I don't feel nearly as satisfied as I know I should feel.

Tessa could give me some answers as to Montica's absence, but I've purposefully steered clear of her today. I kissed her, and I don't know how I can face her after that. How does she feel about it? How do I feel about it?

"It l-looks like s-something," Ritchie declares, stepping away from the center's front wall.

I follow him, taking a few steps out into the lawn. The project is steadily approaching completion, and for the first time, it actually looks like the vision Ritchie shared with me. The iron bars, the sheets of plywood, and other miscellaneous materials have finally formed a circle—our Earth. Well, it's a stretch to call it that yet.

"And it's good timing," I respond, placing my arm over his shoulder. "Don't you have a job to get to?"

Ritchie laughs. "I'll g-get m-my stuff."

Two minutes later and we're walking down Ferry Street, downtown Lafayette stretched out before us. Roman called me last night and asked if I'd show Ritchie to the shop. Initially, I didn't want to do it, but I found a benefit in helping him. Yesterday was about Ritchie. Today, it's back to me. Or so I've tried to tell myself.

Another five minutes and we're standing in front of Gerhard Antiques.

"W-wish me l-l-luck."

"You don't need it," I respond, pushing him toward the door. "Break a leg."

He waves, then disappears inside. I know he'll be a great help. Actually, there could really be no better help. He'll earn his minimum hourly wage in fifteen minutes, because he's everything that I'm not, and then some.

I'm sure Roman and Eliza wouldn't mind seeing me, but I look like crap. I'm sweaty and still partially buzzed from the whiskey in my "break time" flask. I move on a few doors down the street.

The Art Studio is much more alive than the last few times I've been here. And there is no chance of me setting off the alarm. The long hall of art is filled with patrons, so much so that I have to squeeze my way through. There was a time when someone would recognize my face from the pictures that accompanied my artwork, and I'd get questions, and even the occasional request for an autograph. But I haven't had a new piece in over a year, and like most fifteen minutes of fame, it only takes about thirty seconds to be forgotten. I've also lost about thirty pounds and look like a skeletal frame of what I once was.

I nod at the new receptionist, who by her star-struck gaze, must be the only person who recognizes me. She's young, tattooed, and a tad revealing in some of her more intimate areas. She must have been a Bob hire. He's been known to hire by primal instinct.

Strangely, my office door is wide open. I can see the stack of mail on the floor, and behind it, my unfinished masterpiece. It's not until I'm in the room that I see Joseph standing in the corner, looking over some papers scattered on my old bulletin board.

"How did you know I'd be here?"

Joseph turns, displaying his always sharp attire—suit and tie, and his standard, overly polished shoes. "Call it a hunch."

"Who'd you talk to?"

Joseph gives me a half-smile. "Eliza was here earlier. She told me you were accompanying Ritchie to his job today. I thought maybe you'd stop by."

"Lucky guess."

"Educated guess, I would say."

I move around my desk and start to study my unfinished work. "You really think the best of me, don't you?"

"Always."

I'm surrounded by people who believe in me—more than I believe in myself. "Can you tell me why Eliza was here?" I don't ever remember her coming to the Art Studio before, unless I had an exhibit.

Joseph sits down across from me in one of the dusty chairs by the door. "You'll recall, there was a time, before your fame caught up to you that you paid for this space. It was only added as a perk after you became a resident associate with the studio. Given your prolonged absence, somebody had to pay for it."

I'm not sure why I didn't realize that before. The realization of his words hit hard, Eliza and Roman, forever taking care of me, believing that I would come back. They've given more than I can truly imagine. I remember when I got Joseph's message about the A.W.A Resource Center project, and how much Eliza and Roman wanted me to do it. They were trying to get me back here, to find something that could bring me back from the dead. And somehow, they've partially done it. However, I've still got one foot in the grave.

"Can I ask you something?"

"I'm all ears," Joseph replies, before crossing his legs in an attentive pose.

"Why do you all care so much about what I do with my life? Why do any of you want me to succeed? Aren't there other people that deserve your attention more than I do?"

Joseph has a look of wisdom in his eyes. I remember the first time I saw it. It was after my first exhibit failed miserably. I don't remember what he said, but his words were the spark that lit the fuel behind my passion. Every exhibit that followed was a success, and steadily my name grew, and my fame skyrocketed.

I guess in a way, I owe my success to him.

"Well, in short, because we see something in you that is good."

"That *is* short for you." I sit down behind my desk.

Joseph laughs. "Well, I plan to give you the long answer. I was just getting you prepared."

I allow a laugh of my own. "By all means, continue." I try my own attentive pose, but it comes across ridiculous.

Joseph relaxes, rescinding his rigid posture. "You know, I've been in the art business a long time. I've worked in galleries in New York, Paris, London, and even a stint in Japan. I've seen talented artists from all over the world, no doubt names that you've heard before. And they've all had a passion—a fire—for their work. That same passion resides in you. When you first started, I saw it, and there was talent and skill, amidst a creative side to you that most artists don't find until later in their careers.

"Even your first exhibit, the one that failed in so many ways, in my mind was a thing of beauty. I still have two of your pieces in my home. That was great work. Sure, the public didn't see it, but I did. The other artists in the gallery saw it. We knew you would be great. We could feel it, even when Bob in his asinine fashion thought differently, I bet all my chips on you, and won."

Joseph's support spans from the beginning. He gave me my first shot just out of college.

He leans in closer to me, resting his arms on his legs. "The passion I saw in you was only the beginning. It was just a shade of what was to come. That day you came in to my office and asked me to hire Jessica. That day I saw a passion that is contagious, unyielding, and inspiring. You begged me to give her a chance, even though she had no qualifications, no experience, and quite frankly, didn't impress me that much in the interview. What I saw that day was love at first sight, and it was a passion that was far greater than anything I'd seen before, and I know it fueled your work later. I don't think without her you would have been as famous as you were. Successful, yes. World-wide famous, no."

It hurts to hear him speak of her. He grew to love her too. He told me once that she was the best hire he ever made, even better than me. She often looked at him like a father-figure, and he to her like a daughter.

"I knew what that look in your eyes meant. I'd felt that before, when I first met my wife. Love that drives you to do crazy things. Love that drives you to make more of yourself."

I've known Joseph for years and this is the first time he's ever mentioned having a wife. I always thought of him as a lifelong bachelor.

"I don't talk about her much," he says, tears forming in his eyes. "I thought about saying something after Jessica died, but even then, the pain was still too much. My wife died four years into our marriage. I was only twenty-six. She fell on ice, a concussion, followed by a seizure and then a week in a coma. It was the hardest week and a half of my life." Joseph wipes away the fresh tears. "I almost killed myself. Twice. God only knows why I'm not dead now."

I would've never guessed any of this. Joseph always seems so put together, so in control. Suicide doesn't fit his persona in the least.

"The love between you and Jessica reminded me so much of what we once had that I couldn't help but encourage you both. I love the work you've done with us, but I love you more as a person. I loved Jessica. You were my family, and I still feel the same way toward you. You are my family. It won't change. In a way, losing both you and Jessica has been almost as hard as losing my sweet Madeline. If anything, it makes me remember the pain of loss even more."

I can't keep my own tears from forming. "I'm sorry."

Joseph takes a deep breath. "I believe that what you've become is only a brief moment in time. I loved my sweet Madeline, and her death nearly killed me. I became what you are now, but I changed, turned my life back around, and I believe that you will too. I will believe it to the grave, whether that be mine or yours."

Likely mine.

"So, that's why I continue to support you." Joseph's teary eyes are almost immediately replaced with a stern, fatherly expression that I've seen so many times. "Now, I'm growing tired of beating around the bush with weak support and sentimental passiveness. I've seen a change in you, Wes. I know you may be fighting the truth, but even you can't deny that you are changing."

He sounds like Tessa. She seems to think that every little small step is a sign of growing change.

Maybe I am changing, but I'll never be the same, the person who had a passion for something, who fell in love, who genuinely cared for people.

Joseph stands up and wipes the dust from his pants. "I'll let you get to it." He looks at the piece before me. "Are you going to finish it tonight?"

He knows my work well. I look down on the piece, and see a few subtle changes, some additions that need to be made, but only a few hours of work left. "I thought about it."

He smiles. "Change, my friend. Seeing you working on this piece is change. You may not believe it, but it's true."

I run my hands over the rusty metal, careful not to cut my hands on the barbed wire. I replace the somber mood with a fake smile. "Are you going to leave me alone so I can finish it?"

Joseph nods. "I will, but I'm afraid I have bad news."

I pull my hand away, but not before a sharp piece of metal catches my skin. I immediately shove my index finger in my mouth, sucking the blood away from the wound. Joseph waits and then leans forward, but when I show no sign of pain, he settles back in the chair. "Montica came in today, she quit the project. She has enough credit to finish the term which ends next week. She didn't give me any specifics, but she also said she called Tessa and gave her notice at the Resource Center. I just thought you should know if you didn't already."

I immediately feel betrayed, a hurt that is different from the usual sting of loss that accompanies me. I don't know what I feel for Montica—not love—something more like a bond between my life and the work that I've been able to accomplish the past month or so, which of course is compounded by lust.

What could have possibly led her to leave? I'm her hero, right? This is the project of a lifetime for her.

I try not to betray my feelings to Joseph. "Thanks for letting me know."

Expecting Joseph to leave, I lean back in my chair, putting my nicked finger back into my mouth. But Joseph doesn't move. There's more he wants to say.

"Just spill it already," I finally say. "You've given me your life story already." The words come out harsh, especially after Joseph's heartbreaking tale. But this news makes me angry, upset, and very frustrated.

"Take this with caution, as I'm not usually the wisest person regarding relationships..." Joseph is actually quite adept relationally, and I've never seen anyone have even the slightest hint of dislike for the old man. "...but, if I were you, I'd probably make it a priority to go and see her before her semester is over at Purdue. She did seem a little distraught when she came in. I called Tessa after she left, and she told me that you and Montica had grown close, whatever that means. I'm not sure where the young lady lives, but most students go back home for the summer, especially ones without jobs."

I'm still a little shocked at the situation, but I can't help but realize how selfish I am. Montica and I had grown close, in some way, but I don't even know where she calls 'back home.' Outside of her love of art, and the physical relationship we developed, I know little about her. But I know enough that I can't let her go without figuring out what's wrong.

"I'll think about it," I tell Joseph, although my mind is already made up. Calling isn't going to be enough. She's clearly ignoring me. I'll have to go to her.

Joseph smiles and politely nods again. "Good." He leaves, closing my office door behind him.

Chapter Eighteen
Answers

I relish Ritchie's unending chatter as he relentlessly recounts his first day of work at the antique store, though his praises of Roman and Eliza do fall on deaf ears. His words aren't untrue, but I'm just not in the mood to hear it.

I'm not in the mood to work either. At odds with my resolve, I did not finish the piece on my desk last night, and I have no plans to get much work done on the Resource Center project today. Normally, Ritchie would question my lack of action, but he's too busy daydreaming about his soon-to-come, second day of work in the world of over-priced old stuff.

Montica's absence wears on me, and Tessa is out of the office again today, so I can't get any further details on the situation. One of the staff said Tessa had another appointment, which calls into question whether or not she's hiding something. I can't help but wonder if her absence has something to do with Montica quitting, if she's busy trying to do what she does best—helping.

When it's finally time for Ritchie to leave for his job, I'm relieved. We didn't accomplish much, but I can at least see some improvement, I think. I watch Ritchie walk down the street after a quick goodbye, and he has an obvious hop in his step.

As I'm picking up the tools, a familiar "hi," removes my attention from the task at hand. Angela stands over me, a smile on her face, baring her crooked teeth. "Hi," she says again.

"Hello," I respond, just as a staff approaches.

"I'm sorry," the woman says, as she tries to corral the young lady.

"Hi," Angela says one more time before complying.

A few minutes later and I'm caught between two worlds. CityBus. I sit beside a man, who if he isn't homeless, has really let himself go, and a suited fellow who probably just left a multi-million-dollar financial firm and is headed for the golf course.

Even in my depressed, anxious state, I can't help but see the irony.

Homeless man wears tattered clothes, so frayed and matted, it's hard to tell where each article of clothing begins and ends. His beard is thick, and there's foreign material matted inside of it. I can smell the alcohol on his breath.

Suited man has the strong scent of some gaudy cologne. His pants are perfectly pleated, his tie centered directly between both sides of his suit jacket, a gold tie clip holding it in place. It's hard to imagine that his garb has been through a day's work, and I imagine that most of his job consists of mental stress, very little physical activity. He's clean-shaven, and could probably try out for a model agency if this career doesn't pan out.

The irony is that I have been both of these men. Before Jessica was taken from me, I was the suited figure. I had everything going for me, and there was little that I felt I could not handle. It was me against the world.

Now, I am the homeless man, bent toward the bottle, hopelessly alone, very little hope for much greater. I may be clean on the outside, but I stink of filth and rot on the inside. That's probably why Montica is leaving. Something I've said or done has exposed my true filth.

Purdue University is busy, kids—I guess adults actually—ride by on bicycles or walk with stuffed backpacks, some ready to start their nights, others dreadfully walking to their evening classes. My stop is filled with students, patiently waiting to take the spots of those who are getting off. I push myself through the chaos, bumping shoulders with both business and homeless man.

Montica's apartment building is surprisingly easy to find, once I get outside of the bustle of the levee, the area that separates West Lafayette and Purdue University from Lafayette. She lives on the second floor, third door on the right. Being a weeknight, it's quite calm in the building, but I can still hear the thud of the bass coming from somewhere.

When I see Montica's door, number 203, I pause. I can feel my hands shaking. I don't know why I believe it, but I'm sure that whatever has caused her to make these rash decisions is big, much bigger than I can handle. I have enough problems to solve on my own, so how can I even dream of helping her carry hers?

I've tried to convince myself these last few weeks that she's just a girl, someone that I used to fulfill my needs. But I know that I'm lying to myself. I went out of my way to show her that she wasn't just that, something that I haven't done for anyone else except Ritchie. I can't say she would ever be more to me than a colleague, or an acquaintance. But at the same time, I can't truthfully claim that we would never be close.

I take a deep breath and force my hand to the wooden door.

In a movie, it would've taken several knocks, and I would have given up. Then, she would've opened up the door just as I had given up hope and was walking away. At least that's how I've always imagined these situations to work.

Of course, this isn't a movie. I barely have my hand pulled away when the door opens.

Montica stands before me, wearing pajama bottoms and a white tank top, which stands out in stark contrast to her brown skin. Her face seems forcefully restrained, her eyes devoid of emotion. Although she lacks the flushed skin, the puffiness underneath her lashes, and the redness that accompanies tears, I just have this nagging feeling that she's cried today. A lot.

"I thought you'd come by," she says, shakiness in her voice.

I try to casually walk in to her apartment, but she stands firm. She places her hand squarely on my chest. "I don't think that's a good idea."

I'm surprised by her curt response and don't have the wherewithal to question her. Instead, I find myself staring at her, taking in the defeated, weak, and strange aura coming off her in waves. Her shoulders seem overly slouched. Her already-thin figure seems thinner. There's just something so different about her, but I can't place my finger on it.

While I'm studying her, Montica bites her bottom lip. She takes one step out into the hallway, effectively shutting me out. "We just need to quit whatever this is. I'm one week from summer graduation and going home, I'm not working with you, and we both know that this isn't going to work out. You don't really care about me. That's obvious."

Her voice lacks conviction, and her words seem planned. *Days of planning while ignoring my phone calls.*

But I do care about her, in some way that I can't even understand myself. "Why?" That's all I can force out of my mouth.

"I just don't want to get hurt." Her eyes shift away as she speaks. She's lying.

I grab her shoulders. "Can you actually look at me and tell me the truth?"

She struggles to match my gaze, and I'm reminded of this familiar situation, déjà vu. There were times when Jessica would refrain from the truth, usually in times when she knew it would hurt me. I would force her to look at me, my hands on her shoulders. Jessica would cry and the words would then flow from her mouth, sharp daggers of reality.

Montica begins to cry too, and for a moment I want to embrace her, but there's a divide that I cannot cross. The tension in her body, a subtle shift away from my own tells me that.

"Whatever it is, I can take it. Just tell me why you would quit everything. The money is good, but you were the one that really won me over for this project. If not for you, I don't think I could have done this." I hear Tessa and Joseph's words in my head, but I struggle to allow their truths to escape my own lips. "I've changed since I've met you. Maybe not a lot, but I've changed."

Montica is now sobbing, her head bowed toward the carpet. "It's not that easy."

What isn't that easy? I just want to know the *why*. Why is she quitting on a project that she had such a passion for? Why is she quitting a job that she said she loved? Why is she giving up on me?

"Just tell me what's going on. Please."

Her tension dissolves. Her body crumbles into mine and I embrace her.

I'm not sure how long we stay in this position, but she eventually pulls away. The tale-tell signs of emotion that were missing earlier are now evident. She is fragile, one step away from a state that I've lived the last seven months in. A depressed state.

I continue to hold on to her shoulders, but I try harder to be less commanding. "Can you just tell me why you are doing this?"

Montica wipes the tears away from her face first before speaking with a noticeably weak voice. "I told myself I wouldn't give in. I told myself that I wouldn't tell you the truth. I guess I'm not that strong."

There are few women as strong as I've come to believe Montica is. Whatever she is going to tell me is severe, heartbreaking, or worse.

"I went to the doctor and they said I was pregnant," she says.

My hands fall away from her, and I immediately feel like throwing up. The word bounces between the walls of my mind, but I can't believe it is truly there.

Pregnant. She's pregnant.

My back is against the uneven wall behind me. Every breath I take seems like it's labored. This can't be happening. I felt this way when Eliza announced her pregnancy, but this is so much closer to home.

"How far along?"

Her eyes begin to glisten again. That thread of sanity in her eyes is shredding away. I see a hopelessness in them that I've seen in my own before. "I said that I *was* pregnant. It was a miscarriage, Wes. I was five weeks along. I wouldn't even have known if I hadn't been feeling so ill."

I can't even empathize with her, because her words have stabbed a hole so deep inside of me that I can't even stand. I slide down the wall, a wave of painful thoughts and memories flooding through me. I can't contain my weak stomach this time, and I gag twice before throwing up the contents of my lunch.

This debilitating pain has not been present for weeks. I have not had to hide myself behind the numbness of pills and bottles for something so heart-wrenching. My addictions have certainly continued, but not because of something like this. Not because of the hopelessness of loss, the futility of life, the shame of guilt.

My baby—dead. I've chosen to hide a similar memory for so long, to bury it so deep down that I've nearly forgotten it. But I can't hide it now. It rears its ugly head in a way so agonizing that I can't ignore it.

"I'm sorry," Montica cries out.

I don't even know where I find the strength to speak. "Why didn't you tell me?" I gag again, but only spit leaves my mouth. I see the tears falling onto the floor just above my mess.

"What would be the point?" Montica yells rhetorically. There's anger behind her despair. "You're a loser!" she continues. "You could never raise a child. You could never be a father. You're a drug addict. No matter how hard I tried to convince myself otherwise, I knew the *real you* hid behind the sweet facade that you displayed. You used me. You don't even know anything about me." She hovers over me, rage in her eyes. "Where am I going home to, Wes? Where?"

I don't know. She's right. I know nothing about her. I did use her.

"North Dakota," she answers for me. "You used me. And you did this to me."

Her voice becomes a hollow ringing in my ears. It's not the first time I've heard those words. They hurt the same now.

"You're right," I finally manage to say.

Montica has her hands over her face. Tears flow through her fingers as she sobs uncontrollably.

But I can't feel her pain. I'm too busy with my own. And that is proof enough of what I truly am.

A monster.

"I'm sorry," I say, but the words are empty.

Montica steps back into her doorway. "It's better this way," she says. "That's what my parents told me. It's better that the baby died, for my future, for its future. What future would it have had with a person like you for its daddy?"

Montica steps all the way back into her apartment. "Goodbye, Wes." She slams the door.

I curl up beside my mess and wail for hours. I cry so hard that my head feels like it's going to explode, that my body aches in ways that I haven't felt in so long. I cry because I know that what I've done is unforgivable. I cry because I can't hide from the memories that have resurfaced.

I can't hide anymore.

At some point, the sound of young people coming up the stairs forces me to get up and leave.

Chapter Nineteen
The Truth of Things

Five ive minutes, or two hours, I haven't a clue, but it's the longest I've ever waited for anything—or so it feels. "What's taking so long?" I holler through the bathroom door.

The door opens, and Jessica stands before me, beautiful in her sweat pants and tank top. She holds out the small plastic stick as if it's a prize I've just won.

"It's not easy when you want me to do five of them." She betrays no emotion.

"So?" I ask, unable to contain my anxiety.

She waves the small stick in front of my chest "You be the judge."

I study the small screen, squinting to see whatever it is that I'm supposed to be seeing. It's hazy, but there are two lines. I immediately feel the disappointment.

She must sense my change in emotion as I stare at the dreaded double lines once again, because she starts to laugh. "I picked this one because I knew it would confuse you."

After several years of hearing the opposite, her words are too hard to take in. "You mean... we're pregnant?"

Tears form in her eyes before she answers. She nods.

Embracing her is the only thing that seems right in that moment. Every hardship, every night of tears, every ounce of doubt is washed away. "You're sure?" I question.

"I did five of them. If that's not sure, then I don't know what is," she says through happy tears.

I can't help but cry myself. There is a relief, a sense of amazement that washes over me. It's greater than any piece of art could ever be. Before this moment, I didn't know I could love her any more. But I do. I love her with every fiber of my being.

There is no fonder memory than this one.

Two short weeks later, and that beautiful memory was replaced by another—one of her body being laid out in a casket, lowered into the cold, wet ground. I'd suppressed that joy for so long, but Montica's revelation has unearthed the pain, the sorrow, the devastation of it all.

It's late now, but I am finally ready to share the agony that I've hidden away. I need to talk to someone that's lived through this pain, and knows, at least in some way, what I'm going through.

Tessa looks tired and surprised when she opens the door. I'm sure the tears in my eyes and my sweat-soaked clothes are cause for concern.

"You again?" Kalen comments as she steps up beside her mother.

Tessa places her hand over her daughter's mouth, but I can hear the muffled curse word between Tessa's fingers. She gives her daughter a stern glare. Kalen rolls her eyes and walks away.

"She was pregnant," I say.

Tessa steps out of the house and closes the door behind her. "I know."

"No, not Montica. I mean, she was. But Jessica was pregnant when she died."

When I look into Tessa's eyes, she seems unmoved by my revelation. She doesn't say a word, and instead wraps her arms around me. I'm sick, I'm depressed, and I'm exhausted. I collapse into her arms and together we fall to a seat on her cement steps. And I sob.

For several minutes, I hold nothing back. Tessa is firm in her embrace, but she stays silent, allowing me to spill out my emotions.

Once I stop weeping, I realize she's wearing shorts and a baggy t-shirt—probably her pajamas. I've inconvenienced her, she was probably asleep, for hours. Her staff said she was gone for an appointment today, so she's probably unwell.

"I'm sorry if I woke you."

Tessa squeezes my shoulders tighter. "Don't worry. I'm here for you." At this moment, that's what I need most. Not drugs, not alcohol, not sex. Just someone to listen.

"She was pregnant."

"Does anyone else know?" she asks in a whisper.

"No," I respond. "I couldn't bear the reminder. I lost my wife and my baby. I lost everything."

"I'm sorry," she says. "And now you lost everything again?"

I'm not sure if she can see my head in the darkness, but I nod. I've lost every child that I've ever made. God is cursing me, I know it. God wants me to wallow in my sorrow, to die a sad human being.

"It's not your fault," Tessa says.

She's wrong. It is my fault. I slept with Montica. I took chances. And now, history is repeating itself. I won't be able to push the memories away again. I won't be able to survive this.

Tessa appears to sense what I'm thinking. "This is part of who you are. You crashed after Jessica's death. You gave up. Now, you have an opportunity to change how you handle this. When Montica came to me, I knew this would be hard. But what you've told me tonight makes it even more real. I lost my child once, but I got her back. You don't have that choice, but you can get *you* back. I know it."

I tear myself away from her comforting embrace. Her words are turning into some kind of pep talk. "I'm gone. I've spit on my wife's grave with my actions. I'm a terrible person. Montica said it herself. *I could never be a father to that child.* Maybe your God took it away from me because he knew that I couldn't be what it needed. Maybe your God punished it because of me."

Tessa doesn't flinch at my accusations. "Could be."

Her words stab at my heart.

"Maybe it's time that you stop with these little improvements you've made and change completely. Don't you think Jessica would have wanted that? Don't you think that your children would've deserved it?"

My children. My dead children.

She's right, but I don't know how to do what she's saying. "Yes, I think that's exactly what I should be doing, but how?"

Tessa wraps her arms around me again. "For starters, stop feeling sorry for yourself and do something. Anything." She releases me and then stands up. "I'm going to go and get a jacket. Then we can take a walk. When I get back, I just want you to talk to me. No crying, just talking."

I'm too surprised by her frank words to respond. She disappears inside, then returns less than a minute later.

My tears are gone, but the pain is ever present.

"Let's go."

It takes two blocks of silence before Tessa speaks. "Tell me about Jessica?"

If she would have asked me that question last night, before all of this, I might've answered it. Yes, I was still broken, but my life was changing. Everyone else saw it, and though I denied it, I could see the change as well.

When I don't answer, Tessa just asks the same question in a different way. "What was your marriage like?"

There's this pit in my stomach, this sick feeling that won't go away. I haven't talked about those few years of marriage with anyone. After her death, Roman tried to get me to go to counseling at the church. I laughed at him. I think it was the only time I laughed until a month ago.

Another few blocks before Tessa stops. She turns to me. "You need to talk. It will help."

"I can't."

"You can," she says.

"No."

Tessa grabs my shoulders. "You have to. If you ever want to get past this, you have to talk. There's a gift in words that sets us free."

That last phrase spins my mind into a memory. Jessica said that to me once, the words taken from her favorite poet, Edward McClage. It happens immediately. I can't help but see Jessica standing in front of me, her voice replacing Tessa's. I know it's not her, but I don't care. Jessica's fake presence is enough for me to allow the words to spill out.

"I was in love with her from the moment I met her," I say.

Jessica—I mean Tessa—starts walking again. I follow her and the words keep coming. "When we got married, I fell in love with her even more. And our lives were like a dream come true. I was famous for my art. She supported me and loved every aspect of what I did. We worked together, and it was amazing. I can't remember if we even fought once in the first year of our marriage."

Tessa turns toward Columbian Park.

"The more famous I became, the more I loved everything about her. We were rich, had fame, but she never changed. We bought a small house in the middle of town. We gave away most of the money we had to charity and her church."

"Your church," Tessa corrected.

There was a time when I would have called it that. But God can't win me back now. He took her, and I'll never forgive Him for that.

"She was so humble, so trustworthy, so loyal. She was everything that I could never be. I needed that. I needed her.

"It wasn't until we started trying to get pregnant that things got bad. After six months of trying, we started to wonder if there was something wrong. We went to the doctor and did tests. Nothing was wrong. In the end, it took us two years of trying, doctor's appointments, different methods, but nothing worked."

Tessa starts walking toward *our* swing set. At this hour, we could probably get in trouble for being in the park, but what does that really matter.

"The lows were really low," I continue, barely taking a breath. "We fought so hard, so often, that I put all of my time into work. I neglected her. I neglected my family. And she let me have it. She told me often enough that I was screwing up, but she was so gracious in the way she said it and so I turned my back on her.

"That isn't to say we didn't have our good times. I loved her, but I just didn't know how to deal with the constant disappointment, the constant letdowns and watching her brave her way through them. I was never as strong as her. I couldn't continue to take it, and it was my fault that our marriage was a mess."

Tessa finds the swings and sits down. I follow suit. For a brief moment, I take in the story I am telling her. This is everything that I never thought I'd share. I'm exhaling the brokenness, and it feels so good to finally let it out.

She starts swinging, but she doesn't say anything. Instead, she looks at me, her eyes telling me to continue.

"It was two weeks before she died that we found out she was pregnant. The relief, the happiness, everything was wonderful. It was like we fell in love all over again. I remember it was like there was nothing in the world that could hold us down. We made love like it was the first time."

I know my cheeks are red, but I'm sure Tessa can't see them in the dark. "The week after we found out was like our honeymoon all over. I remember Joseph asking if I was okay at work. He could tell something had changed. But we didn't tell anyone. With all the heartache and pain that it took to get to that point, we didn't want to take chances with sharing the news and then running into complications with the pregnancy. We did, however, go to the doctor to make sure everything was good. We found out that we were six weeks along, much further than we thought. We celebrated that night with dinner and a movie, a much-needed date after two years of arguing and bitterness."

I pause to collect my thoughts. I'm to the part of the story that hurts to think about. The part that has led me to this desperate place in my life. The pain in my chest starts again, and I can't help but place my hands on my stomach, as the pit forms inside of it again.

Tessa reaches over and grabs the chain on my swing, holding onto it until she comes to a stop. "I know this is hard, but keep going."

I take a breath. "And then God took her away from me. She died. My baby died. I lost everything."

"Why didn't you tell anyone about the baby?"

"I just couldn't. Everyone was so busy talking about Jessica, and I had to go through the pain of that. I couldn't add the pain of everyone talking about the baby as well. I chose to hide it because I'm weak."

"That's why you got so upset when you found out Eliza was having a baby?"

I nod. "It's the first time I've dealt with the memories. I was able to suppress the full burden of the pain then. But now, after tonight, I couldn't hide it anymore."

"I'm so sorry," Tessa responds. "I am so, so sorry."

I heard those words a lot after Jessica's death. They do nothing for me. "What is there to be sorry for?"

She doesn't respond. "You're right. It's not my fault." I can see her cringe at the bluntness of her own words. She starts to swing again.

For a few minutes, I just watch her, wordless. I can't believe I've bared my soul. I bottled the pain up, allowing it to control me for so long, and now I see that suppressing these feelings is what forced me to numb them.

"How do you feel?" Tessa finally asks.

Hurt. Depressed. And sadly, stone sober. I could use drugs, any drugs right now. But in a way, I do feel relieved. The pain is no less present, but allowing someone else to share the burden is liberating.

"I feel better. But it doesn't change who I am."

"Who do you want to be?"

"Not the person Montica said I was."

Tessa stops swinging. "And that's what it comes down to. That's what's really bothering you."

"Of course it is. When Montica said that it was better for the baby to have died than for it to have grown up with me as a father, I knew it was true. I'm a terrible person and I don't deserve to hold the title of daddy. I don't deserve anything good in my life.

"I've been hiding behind this bravado of not caring, but I do care. I want to change," I cry out, much louder than I mean to.

Tessa is next to me before I collapse back into her arms. "And you can. I know you can. That's why I'm helping you."

I hold onto her as hard as I can, shaking away the urge to cry like a two-year-old child with an ugly abandonment. "But I don't know how to change."

"And neither did I," Tessa says. "Neither did I, but God helped me through it. And you have to help yourself too. You can't keep going back to the drugs and alcohol. You have to separate yourself from that life. I'll help you. Joseph will help you. Your family will help you. You can't get Jessica or those precious little ones back. You won't be able to undo what happened to Montica. But you can use the rest of your life to be something else. Something better."

Again, she's right. I know it. I pull away from her embrace. For some strange reason, I expect to see Jessica's face staring back at me again. But she's not there. I see Tessa's beautiful appearance, her dark hair against the black night, her dark eyes set against her beautiful pale skin. I see compassion in her eyes.

She's always helping someone. Kalen's words. It sounded naïve and ridiculous to me then, but now, I can't imagine anyone else I'd want on my side.

I know what I have to do. I can see the steps I need to take.

Tessa just stares at me, waiting for a response. She grins, then quotes McClage again. "'There's a gift in words that sets us free.' So, say something."

She sounds so much like Jessica. I'd almost forgotten how I'd kissed her at the front door of my brother's house. It was because she reminded me of my wife that day. Now, I see so many similarities in the two that I can hardly wrap my mind around it. And maybe, that's why I tried to push her away after I met her. Maybe, that's why I can't seem to stay away from her now.

I kissed her then, but tonight, I don't feel that same sudden passion. I'm only grateful that she has invested so much in me when I've given her nothing in return.

She's looking for words, but there are none to express how thankful I am for her at this moment.

Edward McClage was right for once. Tessa's words are certainly a gift.

Part 2
Awake

Chapter Twenty
Letter

Jessica Lynn Gerhard died November 27th, 2015 at twenty-six years of age, a lifetime of memories still ahead of her. God took her away from me, along with the child in her womb, a child that was the answer to years of struggle and desperation, hundreds of hours of prayer and tearful begging.

I remember that day so vividly. Partly because I relived it a thousand times the week after she died, and partly because it was the last normal morning of my life. I woke up that day, her beautiful eyes staring back at me, a glow on her skin, the glow that came with knowing our dreams were coming true.

That is my last truly happy memory. I kissed her, told her I loved her, and she responded in kind. Thirty minutes later, amidst the bustle of showers and breakfast, we argued. It was silly and trite and the first fight we'd had since conceiving. I can't even remember what it was about, but I do remember how Jessica left the house that day, the last words that fell off her lips.

"We'll finish this when I get home."

I didn't even respond. I wordlessly watched her leave, thinking she'd be gone for several days, not forever. If only I'd ran after her. If only I'd apologized. Maybe those few minutes would have been enough to change the outcome, change what has become of this life.

It was a Monday, and she was off to visit her parents in Kentucky, to share the good news. We hadn't told anyone yet, and she wanted to tell them in person. I thought it was ridiculous. A phone call would have sufficed, but she was adamant.

I remember watching her car pull away, that little red Chevy.

Three hours later and Joseph's ashen face appeared in my office doorway. I still remember the sinking feeling in my chest, the immediate nausea in my stomach. He didn't even have to say a word. I pulled my hand away from the piece I was working on, that unfinished work of barbed wire and iron.

Joseph cried as the words spilled from his mouth. "There's been an accident. She's dead, Wesley. She's dead."

And I've been dead ever since.

That Chevy barely looked damaged. They said it flipped multiple times, but you couldn't tell from the pictures. There was no dramatic crash, no pile up, no hazardous road conditions, no malfunctions. There was no explanation at all. The final report said that she lost control, but there was no definitive reason as to why.

God killed her. That's the only explanation I can come up with. And I said to hell with the condolences and the well-wishes. To hell with my family, my friends, and to any sense of divine power.

The newspapers called my fall a "colossal collapse to a bright future" after my shows were cancelled, and after I destroyed several of my installations around the city with a sledgehammer. They were right. It wasn't two days after she was gone that I started numbing myself. Pete became my savior, and the drugs, the alcohol, and eventually, the cheap women, they became my god.

I forsook everything from my past, yet tortured myself with the reminders of it—the pictures, the untouched bedroom, the pieces of her that I have not touched, some that I have.

But one piece that I've kept at arm's length. Unable to move, but never far from my mind.

One sealed envelope, that letter that remains unopened, one part of the past that remains in its virgin state. It was in the car, addressed and stamped, ready to be mailed. I'm not sure why Jessica took it with her. God knows I wish it was destroyed in the crash. She died, but something so frail and meaningless survived without a tear. Jessica had told me about a friend she wrote to. They exchanged letters, old-fashioned correspondence that made no sense to me. I didn't know the woman—still don't. I never asked. I never cared. I'm not sure if I'll ever know.

It's nearing eight months since her death now, but as I hold this unopened letter in my hand, the strength to open it fails me. If only she'd put a name above the address, save my heart the pain of opening the envelope, the pull to read the last words she wrote down. I can't bear the thought of hearing her voice in my head, imagining her hands around the pen, the intensity in her eyes as she bared her soul to this friend.

Until now, the letter sat on her nightstand. That's where I left it the night after her death, after a young policeman gave it to me—the last viable piece of my Jessica. I couldn't share it, not even with myself. I'm not sure why I feel it calling out to me now. I spent the last two hours in Tessa's arms, wordlessly wrapped in her embrace. I already said what I needed to. Jessica died, taking the life we created together with her. This haunting memory spurned by God taking the life inside Montica. I told Tessa everything. And she responded.

And for once, I'm listening.

I put the letter in my pocket and look around the room. For the first time in over seven months, I'm in *our* bedroom for longer than a minute. I grab a backpack off the floor that I once used to carry my tools. In the closet, I pull out clothes that I haven't worn since she died, clothes that I didn't think I'd ever wear again. The ones that remind me of her—of dates, first times, and gifts. As quickly as I can, I stuff the clothes into the backpack and leave. If I don't do this quickly, I won't do it at all. When I'm done, I walk past the painful memories hanging next to the staircase and straight outside.

I'm not sure what time it is, but it has to be after midnight. Lafayette is quiet at this time, and my neighborhood is exceptionally calm, save the sound of police sirens in the distance.

I walk as fast I can through the brisk air, constantly telling myself to continue. There's a pull in the other direction, especially when I reach the corner of Kossuth and 9th Street. One way leads to Pete's, the other way leads to my salvation. I nearly have to tear my eyes out to start walking down 9th. I need a hit so badly that it hurts. But the sound of Tessa's voice in my head beckons me to push forward.

Several barking dogs announce my arrival to Lafayette's historic neighborhood. When they stop, the quiet is unsettling here, only the sound of rustling leaves as the wind blows through the crowded mess of historic mansions.

Roman and Eliza's gaudy home looks daunting at night, one of those nightmare images to an imaginative mind. I would have never guessed them to be awake, but there is one single light on. My guess is the kitchen as it's just a dim glow from the dining room window.

I take a deep breath. This is my last chance to change my mind. I could turn around and forget about tonight. I could find a way to hide the pain like before, to add Montica's revelation to the list of painful memories I keep under lock and key. I could find enough booze and drugs to put a blanket over it all.

I see large shadow in the window. Roman.

The figure disappears and moments later, the front door opens. Roman takes one step down. He's wearing a hoodie and sweatpants, and beneath the dim light above his door, his tired eyes meet mine.

I'm standing under a street light, obviously out of place in the middle of the night. There's no turning back now.

Roman takes another step down as I walk the small cement path that winds up to his house, connecting the enormous structure to the driveway. "How did you know I'd be here tonight?"

"I didn't," Roman answers. "I woke up and was getting a drink of water. I don't know why I looked out the window, but I'm glad I did."

There's nothing obviously comforting in his words, but I feel a rush of relief flow through me, matching the cool breeze against my back. I stop, dropping my bag on the ground. "I need help."

Roman smiles. "I'm here."

Usually, he's all over me, the big softy that he is. But this time, I can't help myself. I wrap my arms around my big brother, embracing him like I've never done before. There have been times like this growing up where I knew my twin was the only solace I needed. And Roman was always there. I'd forgotten that. But now, his strong grip is the most comforting thing in the world.

And for a moment, I know things are going to be okay.

Chapter Twenty-One
The Afterlife Two

"Suffering is like dying. Only death gives some reprieve.
Without Your help, I cannot bear it. I'd rather die than go
through this alone. Help me in my despair."

~Edward McClage

It pains me to say this, but my friend McClage was right on this one. He must have suffered some great injustice, or was the victim of some terrible loss. To share my sentiments so clearly, he had to have been through a portion of the suffering that I have; he had to have shared in the same type of haunting memories. Something in his life is shared in mine, whatever that may be.

It's been two weeks since I took a drink, nearly the same span of time since I did a line. Two weeks of a waking nightmare. Fever. Chills. Vomiting. Little sleep. A slowly decreasing appetite for these self-medicating killers. All in a day's work.

Rinse and repeat.

But I'm finally feeling alive. Of course, that doesn't mean that I've made it. I haven't left my brother's home, so I haven't faced reality yet. I haven't faced the option of going home and starting a new life, or turning down 4th Street and heading toward Pete's. Honestly, I'm not sure what I'd choose at this point.

As my desire to be numb slowly subsides, my mind more clearly understands what is occurring. I lie awake at night wondering what Montica is doing. Has she gone back home yet? Has she told her parents what happened? Does she hate herself for allowing me to come into her life? To make love to her. To ruin her. I'm torturing myself, I know.

It's nearing midnight now, and my eyes are glued to the crown molding above my head. The ornate design, superimposed above the antique bedposts are everything that my life is not. Beautiful, organized, mature. Everything about this gaudy room is the antonym of me. Maybe that's exactly what I needed. Who knows?

Tonight, I had dinner with my family. The reprieve between episodes of nausea and fever is much longer now, and I haven't lost my dinner in a couple of days. So, it was time to at least make an appearance.

Steak and eggs, one of my favorites from my life past—actually, my childhood. I'm sure it was my mother who made the suggestion, along with the thought of decorating the guestroom like my room back home.

I'm thankful for the small talk, the shop talk, the anything-but-Wes'-withdrawals talk. There was no mention of my circumstances at all. Even my mother, who helped Eliza cook my *favorite meal*, was able to keep her all-too-often, prying questions at bay.

If there was any moment of pain, it was the quick sting of realization when I saw the small bump under Eliza's blouse. She's barely showing now, and there's a glow about her that reminds me of those two weeks before Jessica died. It was a glow that I didn't get to see on Montica.

I long for the happiness that Roman and Eliza share. That all too elusive feeling McClage wrote about. I'm not sure if what I see in my brother and his wife is true, or if it's a false image created by the masses to hide the truth of pain, but even if it's the latter, I'd take it. I'd take the theory of happiness and all the faults in reality that come along with it.

But I'm not sure how to find it.

Tessa seems to think she has, but it's hard to know if what she believes in is for me. I can't place my misery in the hands of the man upstairs. As tyrannical as He has been to me, I still don't think it warrants Him taking on my life, my pain. I don't want to give Him the satisfaction that comes with control anyway.

Tessa makes it harder to discredit her convictions when she's so freaking kind, so persistent in her love. I see Jessica in her kindness. It's irrational, illogical. But every night she's called, and even between my bouts of vomiting, she's encouraged me. She's been on the other line for hours, just listening to my dark thoughts, allowing me to spill out my demons.

And in a more practical sense, she's been the liaison between the Art Studio and A.W.A. Resource Center. I was a few weeks from finishing the project, which means I'm two weeks behind now. I know Joseph couldn't care less about the deadline. I'm sure my stint in family rehab brings nothing but joy to the old man, but Bob—that fat slob—is probably somewhat ill-tempered by my absence. I hope it's really pissing him off, each day that I don't show up for work.

I could fall asleep to that happy thought if not for the sudden urge for a hit and that strange knocking noise in my head.

Well, it's not in my head. It's outside, or close to me.

I should be angry by the persistent knocking, a once faint noise that has steadily grown stronger. I originally think it the wind, or some haunted noise from an aged house. But the steady rhythm and growing intensity stirs me from my thoughts, the thoughts that keep my eyes open and glued to the ceiling.

The window is as ornate a window as I've seen. It's pompously positioned in the middle of the wall, fashioned in a Renaissance manner, lacking insulation and a pain to open. There's just enough light from the alley to cast a shadow. Two figures, both atypically small. I should be scared by the sight, the possibility of criminal intruders, but the stature of the shadows has me laughing. It's a tired laugh, one that reeks of insomnia.

"Who is it?" I ask, not too loudly. Roman and Eliza's room is just across the hall.

I don't initially get an answer, but instead receive a couple more knocks, which only amuses me more. I roll myself out of the over-sized bed and stalk toward the large window. "What do you want?" I ask, once I'm leaning over the large pane.

The shadows move and a familiar voice strains a whisper through the glass. "Can you open this beast?" Kalen asks.

"Why are you here?"

"Ouch!" The smaller shadow on the left moves erratically. "What is that? Move over." More movement forces the shadows together into one unrecognizable block of darkness. "Stop moving over."

After a few more angst-filled commands and shuffling, I tap lightly on the glass. "Can you answer my question?"

"What question?" she whispers.

"The obvious one."

"Be patient. I brought a friend over to see you. Say something." The last command is clearly not directed toward me.

"H-hi, Wes. It's R-Ritchie. I-I-I—"

"Just wanted to see you," Kalen interrupts. I can hear her impatience. "Can you open the freaking window?"

I groan. "It's a real pain. You're lucky Ritchie's here with you, or I would've just left you out there."

"Real funny," Kalen says. "Shhh!" Ritchie's contagious laugh booms through the quiet.

Instinctively, I turn to my door, hoping he's not too loud. After a few seconds, I turn back to the window and start to crank it open. It creaks in agony, the antique and splintered wood crying out into the night.

I see Kalen's face first, a cocky smile across her otherwise cold face. "It's about time," she mutters.

"H-h-hi," Ritchie says, waving awkwardly.

His smile is contagious. "What are you doing here?"

Kalen begins to climb in. Her long, slender legs are wrapped in black jeans, and she's wearing a black hoodie to match.

"You couldn't have worn something that didn't make you look like a thief?"

She wipes the dust away from her clothes, then stands up straight. "Says the drug addict."

"Former."

"We'll see."

I help Ritchie over the windowsill and he settles on a leather couch to the left of the window, breathing heavily. "Y-y-you missed a g-good c-concert y-y-yesterd-day," he stammers.

"Did you kill it?" I imagine him up on stage, belting out songs stutter free.

"T-totally."

Kalen walks around the room, eyes wide at the extravagancy of the space. She runs her hand across one of the nightstands. "This place is ridiculous."

"I agree completely, but can you tell me why you're here in the middle of the night?"

"He wouldn't stop bugging everyone about seeing you." She points at Ritchie. "Your brother kept saying no, and then he asked Mom, and she said the same thing. So, we made a deal. He introduces me to the guys in his band, and I get him here to see you."

"How old are you again?"

Kalen frowns. "Fourteen. So what?"

I turn to Ritchie. "How old are they?"

Ritchie shrugs. From what I can remember, his band mates were adults, if not, near adulthood.

"Age is just a number," Kalen flippantly says. She smiles but doesn't seem real convicted by her words.

I shake my head. "Whatever." I turn to Ritchie. "Well, you're here. What can I help you with?" I try to sound annoyed, but frankly, I'm a little relieved to have someone here to fill my sleepless night.

Ritchie regulates his breathing, then responds. "W-when are y-you c-c-coming back?"

"To work?"

He nods vigorously.

"I don't know," I answer. "Do you miss me?"

He nods again. "Every d-day."

I can't help but laugh. My response doesn't reflect the emotions I feel inside. The feeling of being wanted, of being missed.

The leather couch gives a little as I plop down beside my friend. "I don't know. I've been through hell and back these last two weeks."

"Yeah, that's all Mom talks about," Kalen says very loudly. She turns toward the door, then whispers, "Sorry, but it's true." She spreads her arms out and falls backward onto the end of the bed.

"She does?" I ask.

Kalen raises her head and eyes me suspiciously. "Yeah, it's weird. You talk every night, right?"

And we kissed. Of course, Kalen saw that too. "It's not like that," I say, a sense of self-consciousness flaring inside of me. It's stupid. She's barely a teenager. Why do I have to explain myself to her?

"Whatever you say, boss."

I flee from the conversation and turn back to Ritchie. "I'm not sure what I can do. What do you want me to do?"

Ritchie perks up in his seat. "C-come b-b-back to work."

My chest sinks with the thought of resuming normal life. I don't know how to leave this safe haven and venture into the world where I've created so much darkness.

"I don't know, Ritchie. I just don't—"

"I n-need y-you to f-finish the p-p-project."

His expression is heartbreaking. "I know, but I'm just not sure if I can do it yet."

"He needs the money," Kalen blurts out.

"What money?"

She sits up on the bed. "Don't be so shy," she says, shaking her head at Ritchie. She turns toward me. "Somehow your friend Joseph got the resource center and the Art Studio to go together to pay Ritchie a little something for his work on your project. The faster you get out of here, the faster you guys get the project done, the faster he gets money, the faster he goes to school."

I can imagine Joseph begging Bob to make this happen, the fat slob giving in just to get Joseph to shut up.

"W-w-well?"

"Is this about you wanting to see your friend or get more money?" I ask, laughing.

Ritchie laughs with me. "B-both."

The laughter must be contagious because Kalen joins in.

And for a moment, I lose track of the plight that is my life, allowing words to come out of my mouth before I can take them back. "How about tomorrow?"

Ritchie looks like he's about to break into song, that look he had on stage when he belted out his own lyrics.

"I know someone else who will be happy about that," Kalen says dryly.

I ignore her, my mind finally catching up with my mouth. It's too late to go back now. "Okay, tomorrow it is." I look between the two. "Now, it's time for you both to get out."

Chapter Twenty-Two
The Stars are not Enough

I got two hours of sleep last night. When I did sleep, my dreams were fluid, mental pictures flowing from one scene to the next like an old View-Master, where the reels were a collection of memories past. Good memories. The type of memories I could get lost in forever.

My eyes open to rays of sunlight and small particles of dust floating through the air, a dull kaleidoscope of miniscule objects, a reflection of my life. Here I am, nothing. A small piece of a vast world.

Once hopeless, but now hopeful.

I know what I have to do. It's not by some profound thought or revelation that I have come to this conclusion. It's by the mere fact that I am wanted. I am needed. I can make a difference in the life of one of the few people who cares about my own lot in this life. I can finish this project and make a mark on this city. I can make a mark on Ritchie's life, helping him attain the money he needs for college, to attain his dreams.

That last part is a half-lie. I can do so much more. I have to do more.

Packing up what little I have with me is easy. It's not until I grab Jessica's unopened letter that I feel a pull in the other direction. But that pull—that pain—is not enough to change my mind, to tear me from the path I've chosen.

Before I leave the room, I catch a glimpse of myself in an old mirror that hangs just above an antique desk on the wall opposite the window. I look different now. Though I lack sleep, and my desire for a crutch is ever present, I don't see the despair in my eyes. I don't see the desperation for another hit. I can even feign a smile, allowing Jessica's favorite features—my dimples—to momentarily dot my unshaven face.

"Where do you think you're going?" Roman asks when I enter the living room. He's wearing a bathrobe, while sprawled out on one of two luxurious leather couches in the room. He has a mug of coffee in one hand, the paper in the other.

"It's time for me to start life again."

He sits up. "Are you sure you're ready?" he asks, trying to hide his concern, but I can already see the sparkle in his eyes. He's always one step away from tears.

"It doesn't matter," I respond. "I have to do this. I have to finish this project."

Roman grabs my arm as I pass, allowing his paper to fall to the floor. "Wait, Wes."

I turn toward my brother, holding a resolve that I did not own two weeks ago. "It's okay. I'm okay."

Roman nods, defeated. "Is there anything I can do?"

Immediately, I think of Ritchie. "You can give Ritchie a raise. Twenty-five thousand dollars to be exact."

He lets go, his eyes growing wide. "Wait? What?"

"Call it a loan."

He shakes his head. "We're doing okay, but I don't have that much money just laying around. We have a kid on the way."

"I'm guessing a boy," I respond. "But that's beside the point. I have twenty-five thousand dollars coming my way when I finish this project, and I want it to go to Ritchie. But the summer is almost over. If he's going to get in this fall, he'll need to get going now."

My brother's wide-eyed gaze turns soft, then his lips form into a smile. "Who are you and what have you done with my brother?"

I'm asking the same thing. "He died."

Roman waves me on. "Apparently so. Go, do what you need to do. I'll give Ritchie a raise. Not twenty-five thousand, but we can talk about that later."

"Thanks."

"Be strong."

I give him my best smile. "I'll try."

As I leave my family's mansion, I feel a rush of relief. I have no need for the money. I genuinely want Ritchie to have it. I need him to have it. If I'm going to change who I am, extra cash won't be of much help. A few weeks ago, extra green meant more drugs, more alcohol. I'm not sure it would mean much different now. I don't know how the temptation will affect me. I'll find that out tonight, when I'm done working and there's nothing left to do but sit around and sleep.

It's abnormally cool for the beginning of August, but the sun's shining, and its heat makes it comfortable.

I walk as fast as I can toward the resource center. It's the opposite direction of Pete's house, and I don't need any more temptation than I already have. I'm sure Ritchie is already waiting, so that's enough of a draw to keep me moving forward.

When I leave the historic Highland neighborhood, the bustle of a workday morning greets me. I follow the long lines of cars heading downtown, congested chaos. In some places, I'm walking faster than the cars are moving, as I force my legs to go, with each step erasing the past behind me. I'm erasing months of grief. Months of depression.

I can feel again, and I can do it without succumbing to the trauma. Running my hands across Jessica's unopened letter, I sigh and with it I release a breath of resolve. Her presence in these unveiled secrets comforts me, and thoughts of her death, the loss of Montica, and the loss of my unborn children still hurt, but are much easier to bear.

When I turn down Cason Street, I can already see the center in the distance, my half-finished work of art on full display. I was hired to do this for a man named Roger. He must have been something else. A much greater man than I will ever be. He persevered through his disability, creating a legend that someone thought was worth one hundred thousand dollars in remembrance.

I may persevere though my own self-made hell, but I'll never know what it feels like to be like Roger. I was once famous for my art, but that means nothing in comparison to being famous for your character.

For being a good person.

Familiar faces are waiting for me. Ritchie's smile is broad, and I can tell he wants to run toward me, but his awareness that it is an inappropriate social interaction is holding him back. I'm sure Tessa told him as much. She stands next to him, where I would have at one point expected Montica to be.

Next to them, Joseph leans against his car, arms folded in front of his sharp suit. He wears a smile to match Ritchie's.

"I'm sober, big deal."

Joseph claps his hands and approaches me. "I'm proud of you." He extends his arms for a hug, his eyes as wet as Roman's were.

"Are you seriously going to cry?" I ask as he embraces me. "Come on."

"When Tessa told me you were coming today, I had to be here to see it. You already look better."

I'm fairly certain I look like crap, but I don't comment. He's my greatest fan and I'm glad for it. I look toward Ritchie. "Hey, you gossip, get over and get this old man off of me."

Tessa nods her permission, and Ritchie tackles me with his own embrace. Joseph barely misses the rough exchange. "Welcome back," he says, retreating. He swipes to hide the tear trail from under his eye.

While Ritchie grasps me tightly, my eyes meet the most beautiful face in the world. At this moment, I can think of no person who I would want to be next to. For some time, Tessa has reminded me of Jessica, but now, I see her as herself.

And for some reason she looks thinner. Tired. But still beautiful. Her smile forces me to disengage from Ritchie. She moves forward as soon as I take the first step.

"You did it," she whispers into my ear as she wraps her arms around me.

"We did it." I grasp her, feeling her pressed up against me. I don't know where the feeling comes from, but there is this closeness, a connection. Secretly, covertly, she's been my rock, the foundation that I've stood on. I don't know how it has happened. It doesn't make sense.

"I would have bet the stars on you. Or at least one night in London," she says.

I laugh. "The stars are not enough, but one night in London is a little high for me."

"Says you," Joseph mutters.

I pull away from Tessa, realizing that our embrace has moved past the length of time it takes for social awkwardness. Joseph has a sly grin on his face.

"Well…" I turn toward Roger's memorial, "… I guess our Earth needs some final touches. We need supplies." I turn back to Joseph and Tessa. "So, which one of you is going to take over where my last assistant left off?" There's a quick pang of guilt when I imagine Montica holding her clipboard, waiting for my command. I shake it away.

Joseph raises his hands. "Don't look at me. I have another place to be entirely."

"Tell Bob he can go die in a—"

Joseph clears his throat, rocking on his heels and walking away. "I'm out. You can tell Bob whatever you want when you come back and start working for us again."

"Deal," I yell at Joseph's back.

He waves before hopping into his car.

"Well, I guess I'll have to do," Tessa says. "I dressed for today, knowing it might be the case." She spreads out her arms, drawing attention to her jeans and t-shirt.

"Okay, get out a notebook. Here's what I need."

I look back at the piece, allowing my mind to venture into a different world. A world where inspiration and delirium coincide—a place my mind was unable to reach in numbed stupor. I see what I need, what things will complete Roger's project.

Chapter Twenty-Three
One Piece of Her

Roger's masterpiece is not yet finished, but there is one project that my hands can bring to completion. It's late, well past the hour for normal human beings. The sky is clear, and a ray of moonlight shines through my office window, revealing the movement of dust on piles of junk. My hands are not my own, moving freely over the medium, iron and steel, a sharp contrast against barbed wire.

This piece is for her, a gift, worthy only of this one person.

I now see her in my dreams. Waking dreams. In the time it takes to walk to the resource center. As I chat with Ritchie on our way to my brother's antique shop. Before I close my eyes each night.

I see her in my work. Even just one piece of her. That's all I need.

From a cursory view of my messed-up life, it'd be a safe guess to assume I'm thinking of my wife, the woman who took both my child and my heart with her to the grave. The woman whose short life should have drained all sense of love that I could carry. Should have. But it's not her any more.

She'll always be there, with a hold on my soul.

But now, Tessa has a hold on me. She grips every fiber of my being. What once was controlled by my depression, and concealed by a drug-induced coma, is now hers.

I think I love her.

No, I know I do.

One month ago, I was at my lowest, now I'm on some kind of strange high. Sober and awake.

And that's why my hands move, ever gently as I sand down the rusty end of one wire. Because I'm inspired, and fueled by passion, instead of the debilitating need to be numb.

It's this passion that rocketed me to fame, the same passion that led to my downward spiral. Controlled, nothing can stop it. Uncontrolled… well, nothing can stop it. It consumes, buries me in this haze of inspiration.

And there is no way to let it pass on its own. The fuel needs to burn off. The destination needs to be reached.

So, it will be.

Joseph left fifteen minutes ago, but not before wetting my shoulder with tears. The old fool just couldn't contain it. "You've done it," he said. "You've passed that point. That point that I had to pass over twenty years ago. The point where you have to let go and live, or you'll just continue to let go and die."

I bowed. "Here I am, alive."

He laughed, wiping away the tears. "I am so proud of you."

I then gave him my best exasperated gasp. "Get out of here before I melt under your affection and praise."

He nodded. "I'll leave you to your work. And I hope to see you here more regularly."

"So would Bob, the idiot that he is."

Joseph barely holds back a grin. "As long as he's making money, he's happy."

More like as long as he's pissing someone off, he's happy. But I didn't share that.

Once Joseph left, I found myself enthralled with the idea of finishing this long-rested piece. It had laid dormant for so long, waiting for me to resurrect it. I'd had flashes— moments where I gave it some breath, but tonight was the final exhalation of life into its metaphoric lungs.

This piece of art will be complete before sunrise. And I have a name for her.

One Night in London.

It's fitting since I plan to give it to Tessa tomorrow. Along with some declaration of how I feel. I don't know how she will take it. If she will take it. But I have no choice. If I don't say something, I may burst into a million pieces. If I don't tell her, I don't think I will be able to live with myself. This newfound life, a life away from the drugs and resentment and depression, and I have the ability to care. Tessa brought me here. She saved me.

I allay those thoughts, and push my mind back into the present, forcing all of my energy into my hands. Into my fingertips. If I plan on getting this done tonight, then I have to work harder, faster.

And so, I do.

***

Saturday comes. In true Indiana fashion, it's one of those unnaturally hot mornings. The sun isn't quite visible over the tiny Lafayette skyline, but the lack of a breeze coupled with the unrelenting humidity means it's going to be a grueling walk.

One Night in London weighs at least fifty pounds, and there really is no way to handle her easily. But that doesn't matter. I have to do it.

When I look at her, I see something beautiful, something significant. The iron bars wrapped in barbed wire and small welded fragments of metal is not a picture of anything. It's abstract, but it's wonderful. Exactly what it should be.

The walk is grueling, but I arrive at Tessa's doorstep at seven a.m. I'm filled with adrenaline and anxiety, but I have the common sense to realize that I'm unfashionably early. It's the weekend. She and Kalen are undoubtedly asleep.

So, I wait on her doorstep, watching Lafayette come alive before me. Her neighborhood is quiet, but eventually cars start passing by, and some of the neighbors make an appearance. The sun peaks over the house across the street.

My mother used to say that the sunrise was a show of God's might. That He was in control of everything. This coming from a woman who faked illness just to see me, it's hard to know if she really believes in an all-knowing being.

I thought I did once. Jessica did. Believed wholeheartedly. Eliza and Roman do. Tessa does. For her sake, I hope Montica—wherever she may be—does.

It seems futile, but the thought of seeing my wife again, the thought of seeing my unborn babies, does seem like a legitimate reason to believe in something greater.

I shake away the thoughts. This is what a mind sans drugs and alcohol can conjure.

I'm not sure how long I've been sitting at her door, but I sense Tessa standing behind me somewhere between the sun completely clearing the houses and the car that passed by without a muffler, completely throwing off the calm equilibrium of the morning.

"You're up early," she says, sitting next to me on the step. "Gee, it's a little hot to be sitting in the sun."

"Yeah, well, it's somewhat pleasant to feel the heat—to feel anything, really." I turn to her and notice a disheveled version of the woman I expected. Dark circles under her eyes, her black hair pulled back in a loose ponytail, revealing some gray at the roots. She doesn't carry the strong stature that she usually bears.

"I haven't had my coffee," she quips, clearly noticing my rude stare.

"I'm sorry."

"It's okay. I'm not always prepared for the day before eight a.m. on a Saturday. Shoot, Kalen doesn't even see the light of day until noon. And we certainly don't expect company."

Although her words make sense, they fall off of me like water. My mind passes over the obvious and burdens me with the weight of her beauty. There was a line from a movie Jessica used to like; one of those one-time-a-year movies. *Pride and Prejudice.* The affluent Mr. Darcy told the protagonist Elizabeth that she had 'bewitched him body and soul.' Or something to that effect.

That is how I feel now. Bewitched, body and soul, but I don't know how to share it. How to put words to the feelings that I have just now come to know myself. Not a month ago these feelings did not exist. I would have thought them impossible.

Tessa half-smiles. "What? Why are you looking at me like that?"

I break her spell, and my eyes find the offering I brought to her. She must follow my gaze because she reaches out and touches the metal contraption.

"Your newest work?"

"My first piece after her…" It's hard to say the words out loud, but I can say them now. "… after Jessica's death."

Tessa places her hand over the top of mine. "Congrats."

I flip my hand over, allowing her fingers to fall onto my palm, before grasping them. "Thank you. For everything."

She doesn't try to pull away and instead matches my grip. "I'm not gonna lie, you had me worried for a while." She turns back to the piece. "It's really beautiful, you know."

"It's for you. It's called *One Night in London.*"

She tries to contain it, but I can see her face blush red. "Is that so?"

I squeeze her hand tightly, just hoping that she won't pull away. "It's the only name I could come up with. It's your dream, I know. The dream of the most beautiful woman I know."

She bites her lower lip. My firm grip is not enough to hold her hand as she pulls away. She looks toward the rising sun. "The great orb of light will pass, but the great orb of love shall never."

She's quoting Edward McClage, that fool.

"The question that lies before us is this…when the great orb cometh to life, will love be a lie or a truth? Or yet, just a fleeting romance conjured by the weakness of fleeting emotions?"

There is little I can say to her words. Part of me hears Jessica quoting them, the only person in the world who can hold his words so highly esteemed. The other part of me knows that they are meant to respond to words that I have not yet spoken.

I cannot say them if they will only be denied. So, I watch the distant horizon with unfulfilled questions, words that I cannot force from my mouth.

"I'm a waste of time," she says coldly a few minutes later.

If anyone is a waste of time, it is me. It *was* me. The words come out before I can stop them. "This piece is for you because I love you, Tessa."

Though she's mostly facing away from me, I can see a single tear slide down her cheek. She reaches for it, but I take back her hand.

"You're crazy, Wes. You've changed, but it's made you crazy. You do not love me."

"I do. And if you don't love me, that's fine. But I do. I do love you. You are the reason I've changed."

She sighs, before turning toward me. Several tears streak down her face now. "I can't return that feeling. I… I just—"

My lips find hers before she finishes her denial. I kiss her briefly, but she doesn't resist. When I pull away, a steady shade of pink appears beneath the water lines on her skin. She smiles for a moment, then her face turns cold.

"I cannot give you what you want. I'm sorry."

There's a sudden sharpness in my chest, but it's nothing compared to other pains I've felt. It bears a resemblance to my family's disappointment, to Joseph's awful tears.

Tessa manages a small grin. "But, I can take my gift and make breakfast."

I nod.

She releases my hand. "I'm sorry."

"I'm not." I did what I wanted to do.

Tessa leans in and kisses my cheek. "I wish I could give you more. But I just can't," she whispers into my ear. "I just can't."

I feel her breath warm on my face as she pulls away.

"That's fine," I respond. "I'll take whatever I can get, and breakfast is a start."

We leave *One Night in London* on the front step and move into the house.

"I thought I heard an annoying voice," a disheveled Kalen says as soon as the door closes behind me.

"Kalen!" her mother sharply scolds her.

Kalen winks in my direction while completely ignoring her rebuke.

"Wes is staying for breakfast," Tessa says. She turns toward me. "Make yourself comfortable and I'll get started."

I nod and plop down on the couch.

As soon as her mom leaves the room, Kalen drops to a slouch on the chair adjacent to me. It's a familiar setting. When I first met Kalen, we sat in the same places in this same room.

She stares at me for a few seconds, her face threatening a grin.

"I was told you slept in until the afternoon."

"I was told you were a loser and would probably never figure your crap out."

I look toward the kitchen, then back to her. "Who told—"

Kalen laughs. "I'm kidding. You know *fixer* in there would never say that. She's too busy *helping* to see reality."

"But you see it?"

She sighs. "Sometimes, but I was wrong about you. You're on the up and up. I gave you like a one percent chance to turn that train-wreck you called life around."

I smile at her sharp words. I gave myself less of a chance. "Thanks for your vote of confidence."

"Anytime." She looks toward the door before her grin melts away. Turning back to me, she leans forward. "You told her, didn't you?"

I give my best confused expression.

"You're not fooling anyone. And you got denied, right?"

Since I'm so easily read, I don't even try to deny it. I nod in agreement.

Kalen sighs, a vulnerability cracking through the veneer. She betrays an emotion I can't quite grasp. "She deserves to be happy, but that's not always an option, is it?"

"Why not?"

She shakes her head. "Never mind. Some people just don't get to be happy. You understand that, right?"

Unfortunately, I do. I've lost more than my share of happiness.

She nervously chuckles. "I'm sorry, that was mean. Don't let me bring you down though. You've been through hell and back and you still have the guts to do something that I can't do."

"And what something is that?"

She raises from her chair. "You've come to terms with reality." Kalen follows with a weak smile. "I'm gonna help Mom finish up. God knows she's never seen me up this early, so why not surprise her again? Besides, she's much better company than you are."

Chapter Twenty-Four
Wild

There are songs that Jessica burned into my head. Strings of words that pop into my mind from time to time, forgotten tunes. Outside of McClage's standards, she sang melodies to all styles of music, from the day's top forty to last generation's lost hits. For every occasion, there just seemed to be a song that accompanied it.

It was just one of the many little things I fell in love with. I was never one for the art of music, but Jessica used to say that "all art forms are part of a greater rhythm in life." I'm not sure what that rhythm of life is, but there's always been something of great force that flowed through me when one of my pieces was born.

One Night in London was the piece I needed in order to tell Tessa how I felt. There's a similar feeling within me now, something I can't really explain. I can't pinpoint with accuracy if it's some type of adrenaline rush or some type of down. I feel like I could run a marathon while at the same time sit back and bask in some form of glory.

There are people everywhere, crowding the small lawn in front of the A.W. A. Resource Center. I see the mayor shaking hands with Bob, who acts like he actually cares about all of this. I hope he doesn't get any words in, or it will be nothing but a long advertisement for the Art Studio. I cringe at Bob's ugly smile as he puffs his chest out at "what he's made."

Behind him, a large sheet covers Roger's memorial, an abstract vision of the Earth, as Ritchie thought best. It looks nothing like my other work because it means more than all of those other pieces put together. I may get a blurb in the paper. "The prodigal son returns. The great Wesley Gerhard is back at it." And that's all it will be. But I don't care. This piece is a mark to something new in my life. A change.

I think Jessica would've been proud.

I get nods and small sentences of gratitude, but for the most part, no one wants to talk to the reformed village drunk. Which is just fine, I asked for it to be that way. Instead, I want today to be about Roger, and in turn, about Ritchie. After all, this was his project, not mine.

My friend looks sharp in his suit, standing next to Joseph and some of the resource center staff. Ritchie basks in the praise and is busy shaking every hand that comes near him. This is his day, in more ways than one.

I feel the twenty-five-thousand-dollar check in my pocket, the one promised to him through a bump in his salary at the antique store. It has my name on it, but this money was never mine in the first place. I never deserved it, and I'm happy that I won't be tempted to use it on drugs and women. God knows how much of each I could have with it.

A few months ago, I would have found out.

The mayor disengages Bob and makes his way to the make-shift podium. Bob flashes a disappointed expression before retreating into the mob.

The mayor checks the mic before clearing his throat. All attention moves forward. "The City of Lafayette has always been a community of hope. We…"

I glance at all of the faces, hoping to see Tessa. But I can't find her. For some reason, she's missing this important milestone. I should feel hurt by it, but I'm more confused than anything. This is her facility. She should be here.

And maybe she is, lost in the sea of people.

There is another absence that tugs at my stomach. In the blanket of mostly light-skinned, Caucasian faces,

Montica's olive complexion is absent. This project is as much hers as Ritchie's. It's my fault she's not here to claim the praise she deserves.

It's been nearly six weeks since she went home. I wonder what she feels about me. Does she hate me? She should. I wouldn't blame her at all if she did. No woman her age should have to go through what she has. No woman of any age should.

It pains me to think about it, but I'll probably never know how she feels. I'll probably never see her again.

I've lost the mothers of both my unborn children. I couldn't stop the first one. That was all the man upstairs. But I take full blame for the second.

The mayor introduces Ritchie, which rouses me out of my pitying thoughts. Ritchie waves wildly, an ear-to-ear grin on his face, not unlike the one he dawns on stage with his band. I don't see the Down syncrome boy anymore. I see my friend, a person who in his life has had much more success than I will ever have.

"Along with the help of Wesley Gerhard..." the mayor points in my direction, and I get a sea of eyes staring at me. "... and Montica Barrough, who is not with us today..."

Thanks for the reminder.

I see Roman and Eliza on the other side of the mayor, standing with a long line of businessmen who are sponsoring some of the resource center's clientele for some other coinciding event. Roman looks dapper, and Eliza glowing, her hands resting squarely on her growing belly.

"So, with that," the mayor booms, "on behalf of the Art Studio, in collaboration with the A.W.A. Resource Center, and the City of Lafayette, I'd like to present to you... *Roger's World* by Wesley Gerhard and Ritchie Filipiak."

The mayor turns toward the building and raises his arms. Joseph and Bob each take an end of the canvas and pull it away. The cloth falls from the façade, and *Roger's World*, in its complete form, is revealed.

Applause fills the air, along with some shouts from Roger's family and friends I suppose. I can't help but smile at the accomplishment.

But the noise fades away as I feel a tug on my sleeve. Angela stares up at me, a flat grin on her face. "Hi," she tells me for the thousandth time. She's in a long dress for the occasion, one that was probably a lot less wrinkled and dirty when she put it on earlier in the day.

As usual, her staff is right behind her, an apologetic look on her face. "I'm so sorry, Mr. Gerhard. Come on, Angela." She grabs the girl's hand to pull her away.

But Angela doesn't budge. With her free hand, she points toward the building, in the general direction of the memorial. "It is beautiful," she mutters.

The young staff woman drops Angela's hand, an expression of shock etched on her face.

"Are you okay?" I ask after she gives the appearance of fainting.

The shock gives way to a smile. "Angela, I'm so proud of you." The woman grabs the girl's hand a second time, then looks toward me. "Mr. Gerhard, those are the first words, other than *hi*, that we've heard Angela say in over ten years. It's nothing short of a miracle. Thank you."

I let the knowledge sink in, but before I can respond, the woman is pulling Angela away and is retreating toward a large group of staff huddled together in the parking lot.

Taking a moment to look between Angela and the memorial that is *Roger's World*, I can't help but think that there are a lot of miracles happening lately.

***

Tessa is nowhere to be found at the unveiling of *Roger's World*, so I give up my search. I haven't been back to my house since I decided to give up the drugs and live once again. Roman's guest room was comfy, but it's time for me to take yet another step forward.

I say my goodbyes—to the few people I know—hand over the signed check, and begin my walk back to my neighborhood.

It's amazing how so much can change in your life, yet some things never do. I look at the houses beside mine, the manicured lawns, the fall decorations, the things that repeat themselves year after year. Although my world has stood still for nearly a year, the rest of the world has moved on. I'm just catching up.

I remember when Jessica and I looked at this house. A two-bedroom bungalow, a perfect fit for a young couple. We probably would've moved had the baby come. Now it's just a mess of a place, overgrown lawn, boxes on the porch, the pit of hell on the inside. I've not yet seen it sober, and I'm afraid it's worse than I remember.

But I push the unlatched door open anyway, smelling the foul air inside. It's dark and musty and hot. Trash is strewn everywhere. I flip the switch, but nothing happens. Apparently, nobody's paid the electricity bill. I know I haven't.

This is what Eliza saw three months ago. A disaster. An embarrassment. The floor is littered with beer cans and pizza boxes, half of the contents still present. I push my feet through the sludge, working my way into the dining room. It's dark, but there's just one sliver of light piercing though the torn curtains. Just enough light to cast a shadow over the figure sitting at the end of the table.

"Welcome home," Pete mumbles.

It takes a moment for my eyes to adjust completely, but only a second to see the foul mood that is conveyed from his downcast eyes. A second later I see his gun resting on the table beside him.

"Hey, Pete." I try to act as nonchalant as possible, but Pete's not an idiot. He can see through my sober duplicity.

He raises his head, and I can see the streaks where tears recently ran their course. "How did you do it?" He looks depressed...pitiful.

"Do what?" I ask, before sitting in the chair opposite him.

He fakes a laugh. "Change."

Love. Family. Both answers will probably lead to him shooting me. I always knew Pete was dangerous, but it's not until now that I truly sense how easily he could end it all. He's put a gun to my face before, he's shaken down a complete stranger for a few bucks, but now I have just a little glimpse of a new life, and I can't help but fear for it.

Pete is the scum of the earth. Not worse than I am, but unenlightened, unable to see the veil that his business—his habits—have placed before him. It's amazing how Eliza so easily dispatched him from my house in what seems like a lifetime ago.

"I had to do it."

He shifts toward me, placing his hand on the table. "You'll never buy drugs from me again," he says, tapping his fingers on the old oak. He meant it to sound like a question, but clearly, we both know it's a statement.

"If you're gonna kill me, you might as well get it over with." I subtly lean away, a deep pit growing in my stomach. I could've said that with such little emotion a month or two ago. But now, I'm afraid. I don't really mean it. It's that one dream again. The one where I die with a bullet to my head. But this time, the theory of happiness isn't so resolute in my mind.

"I'm more concerned with how you did it. Give me something. There was a time that I thought I could change, but then I realized I was meant for this hell. I was born to wallow in the filth of this city. I thought you were born of the same mold, born to wallow along with the rest of us after your wife died. And it pisses me off that you've found a way out."

"I'm sorry," I say, the words barely choking out of me. "I don't have answers. At least not yet. But I'm trying to figure it out."

Pete grips the gun tightly.

I quickly scan the room, but the only weapon I can find is a fork sticking out of a pizza box on the floor.

"I cried today," Pete continues, pointing the gun toward the streaks on his face. "I haven't done that in years. My wife does the crying. I can't stand it. I try to beat it out of her, but that's something that's innate in women. It's not natural in men. But I did it anyways, and I'm angry about it, Wes. I'm angry at you, because you caused it. You made me do it."

I try not to draw attention to the fork, but it's hard to completely pry my eyes away from it. I can feel the sweat beads running down my temples.

The gun is now pointed toward me.

"I'm sorry, Pete. I don't know what else to say."

There's a rage in his eyes now, the same rage I saw the first time he shoved a gun to my forehead. The same rage I saw when he broke Bill's nose. He looks maniacal, crazed. He wants answers and I can't give them to him.

I'm frozen to my chair, but my mind tells me I have to move. I will myself to lunge for the fork. The cold metal hits my palm and I hear Pete yell, his chair slamming into the wall behind him.

Everything is mechanic now, automatic. With fork in hand, I swing wildly into the general direction of my assailant. I miss, and briefly lose sight of him, as he retreats away from the window and into the shadowed corner of the dining room.

He yells some unintelligible phrase, followed by a string of curses. I swing toward his dark figure, knowing that his gun is pointing at me. I briefly see the dark metal. I hear the surreal sound of it firing. And I feel an intense weight hit my left shoulder.

A miniscule moment later I sense pain, along with the disgusting feeling of the fork penetrating his skin. We yell in unison.

Another shot. I hit the littered hardwood floor. It's dark. I can't see him, but I hear footsteps along with a gurgling sound I can't place.

Then, all my senses are engulfed by the flames I feel inside of me.

Chapter Twenty-Five
Hospital Food

There's this memory I'll never forget where the ocean was spread out before us. The smell of the salty air filled our nostrils while the ocean breeze rushed against our skin. It was the 4th of July and it was our anniversary. She was standing before me like a perfect statue cut from the finest marble. She hummed some simple tune, a song I didn't know. Her pale skin shimmered under the sun, sweat glistening. The backdrop of the horizon encompassed her, and I remember just staring in awe. *God must be generous* I thought. Because there's no life where I would have ever deserved this woman.

Just as that thought entered my mind, she glanced over her shoulder. It's as if she knew what I was thinking. And her smile told me I was wrong.

All else faded away. And for that moment, there was no beach. There was no ocean. No sound of the waves, no sensation of the breeze. There was nothing else at all.

It was only us…

I wake briefly to the sound of sirens and frantic voices. Two white faces. Male. One larger than the other, sweating profusely. He curses, then says my name.

I catch the other one's eyes for a moment. But the space around him quickly grows dimmer. I hear my name again, just before everything goes black.

She's still on the beach, glancing over her shoulder. That same smile. I've never felt happier.

***

My mother is by my side every time I wake. She just sits here as if she won't ever see me again. She's lucky. I was shot through the shoulder, not the heart. Clean through. The other shot scraped my calf muscle. Probably won't even leave a scar.

Pete wasn't so fortunate. Fork to the neck. He bled out on the street in front of my house. That block will never be the same for my neighbors. They looked out of their windows to find a bloody mess on the concrete. It will be a place of legend to the local children.

No charges. The officer, off the record of course, whispered into my ear. "He won't be any loss. We've been trying to put him away for some time. You did the world a favor."

He may have been right, but I don't feel good about it. Pete was the only friend I had for six months. Pete was a loser, but with him gone, there's a hole left. He was all I knew after Jessica died. He comforted me at times, offering drugs and women. He scolded me when I wasn't doing it right. He showed me a side of life that I wholeheartedly embraced. I hate him, but there's still a void.

I wonder how his family will respond. Will his wife cry for him? Will she be happy? I can't imagine his death not being a positive in the life of his children.

Too many thoughts. Makes my head hurt. I stop thinking and return to reality.

I may not face charges, but there will be counseling, questions, and some mentor-type person from a local social service program. But if that's the worst I get for taking a man's life, then I'm lucky.

Dad's getting a bite to eat and Mom's glued to my arm, her head resting peacefully on the bed beside me. She looks uncomfortable, hunched over on the chair, but she's been up all night, so the sleep is needed.

"They'll keep you for another day," Roman says before I can even see him. He comes around the small bend in the room holding a silver balloon. He catches me rolling my eyes. "Eliza had to send her love somehow. She's not been feeling well. Our little one is putting up quite the fight."

"Like her uncle?" I'm not sure if it is a she, but that's what I guess now.

"How are you feeling?"

"I was good until I saw that shirt." Roman's bright yellow t-shirt stands out against his extremely tan muscles.

Roman ties the balloon to the bed. My mother stirs a little. "It's a new shirt," he says, a thin smirk on his face. "I ordered you some food on my way up."

My stomach isn't ready for it. Hospital food.

Roman pulls a small stool over, and I can already see that look on his face. The one he gets right before some emotional lecture. "God saved you, you know."

"No, I saved me. I stabbed Pete. God didn't."

"Not just last night. But this whole change in you. Don't you see that?"

I want to argue that it was Tessa, him, and Eliza who helped change me, not the man upstairs, but I'm in no mood to argue, so instead I nod. I can tell Roman wants to say more, but he lets his preaching die, content with my half-hearted response.

He shifts, pulling out *the* letter. *Her* letter. "I found this in your things when I was packing your hospital bag. I—"

"Don't open it!" I yell, pulling it out of his hands. Jessica's letter is meant to stay sealed, the last untouched piece of her.

My mother wakes and stares between us for a moment, dazed. "Hello, baby," she says to her larger-than-most son. Roman embraces her.

She turns to me and pats my hand, an overly sympathetic look in her eyes. "I think I'll go get something to eat."

"Dad's already down there," Roman replies for the both of us.

She stretches and heads for the door, over dramatizing her achy gait.

"I'm sorry," I whisper as the door closes. I trace my hands over the white paper, stained from age and abuse.

"I wouldn't open it. There's only an address, so I wouldn't know who this was for anyways. Do you know?" Roman says.

My heart aches for a moment as I picture Jessica sitting at that desk in our dining room, writing the address on each one of her letters. "I have no idea."

Roman cups his chiseled jaw between his hands. "You're not curious?"

I'd be lying if I said I wasn't. But I don't have the strength. There's just something in me that can't do it. It'd be like letting her go. In my illogical state of mind, it's been the last mystery keeping her alive.

I shake my head, tracing the slight ridges of the ink with my fingers. "I don't know if I'll ever be able to open it."

"That's okay," Roman assures me. He sighs, then straightens on the stool. "You know, Jessica was a great woman. We all loved her. And, as much as I hate to say this, I'm not sure how I would've handled it. Sometimes I wonder if I would have done the same thing as you, especially now with the baby…"

I feel the sting of his words. Roman doesn't know that Jessica was pregnant when she died. Only Tessa knows that part. I want to tell him, feel more of the weight drop off of me.

"… without Eliza I'm not sure how I could live. We're human, Wes. We have deep emotions. And you know me, mine run a little further out on my sleeve."

"And that's why we need God," I interject before he continues.

Roman nods. "You know me well."

Too well. I've heard this spiel before. "Jessica believed in Him. And so do I, Roman. That's what makes it so difficult. I feel He took her away from me. The only thing I had that made me feel alive. He stole my life. And I hate Him for it."

Roman winces at my harsh words. "That's where I think you're wrong. There are other things. Jessica isn't what made you—you. Sure, she was a big part of it, but I saw life in you long before she ever came along. We're twins. I think I know you pretty well. You had your art. You had a desire to succeed. A drive. A passion."

I can't argue with him. I felt that passion when I picked up the piece for Tessa. I started to feel it with *Roger's World*. Joseph said he saw it. Roman saw it. Even Jessica told me she saw it. It drew her to me.

I'm saved from admitting he's right by the sound of the door opening. My mother's humming long before she enters my view. She wears a large smile. "Look who I found wondering the halls," she says.

Kalen enters first, her hand outstretched behind her, seemingly dragging Tessa along. Tessa looks tired, almost fragile. But she is beautiful as ever.

"Hey dude," Kalen says. "Never bring a fork to a gun fight."

Sharp eyes all point to her, none sharper than Tessa's.

She smirks. "Sorry. Too soon?"

My mother giggles, cutting the tension, although she's as appalled by Kalen's words as any. "Well, I'm gonna go find that food now. I'm starving."

Roman stands up and nods. "I'll join you, Mom. Nice seeing you, Kalen, Tessa," he says as he walks by them.

When the door closes, Kalen laughs. "Does he always wear such ridiculous clothes?"

"Always," I'm quick to respond.

Tessa rolls her eyes and then settles them on me. "How're you feeling?" She loosens her grip on Kalen before sitting down where Roman was moments ago. She puts her hand on mine, and I immediately feel alive.

"Like a man that's been shot."

"You look like crap," Kalen says. She sits on the small sofa under the window.

I look to Tessa for a rebuttal, but she grins. "You really do."

"Thanks. Greatly appreciated. I'll have Roman doll me up the next time you see me. Maybe borrow one of his shirts."

"You could stand to borrow some of his good looks," Kalen adds.

I want to laugh, but I know my wound will hurt if I do. "How's Ritchie doing? I didn't get to talk to him on his big day. He was too busy soaking up his fifteen minutes of fame."

"Shoot, he gets that every time he gets on stage." Kalen huffs. "Freakin' genius with a mic."

That's true.

"It was your big day as well," Tessa says.

But she wasn't there. *Why wasn't she there? What could have been more important?* I know I just killed a man, but at this moment, her being gone is a more pressing matter.

"I'm sorry I missed it," she seemingly responds to my thoughts.

"Where were you?" I clutch her hand, as if asking her this question will scare her off.

Tessa's lips are pursed, but she remains quiet. Kalen has no issue answering for her. "She had a doctor's appointment. That's why we're here."

Tessa turns to her daughter, who slinks down in her seat as if she's been scolded. I've been on the receiving end of Tessa's gaze. It's formidable and beautiful at the same time.

But what is she hiding? "You were here all day?" I look at the clock. It's been twelve hours since the ceremony.

"Yes."

"What for? And why do you have so many doctors' visits?"

"I don't."

I can think of at least three missed days at work, and how many times while I wasn't working on the project. Not to mention, she looks different—tired and frail.

"So, what for today? And this is a hospital, not a doctor's office."

Tessa breaks my gaze, but doesn't readily respond.

"It was the doctor's office today, but she needed some blood work tonight. And one of her clients was admitted earlier, so she wanted to visit him."

Kalen's explanation seems too rehearsed. And it's eleven o'clock at night, well beyond visiting hours.

"What's the client's name?"

"Jamie Bridges," Kalen answers.

I make a note to have Roman check up on the claim.

Tessa pulls her hand away from mine and stands. "We should probably get going and let you get some rest."

"You don't have to," I say. "No more questions."

Tessa smiles. "It's been a long day for us too."

I sigh loudly, hoping she sees my disappointment. I wish she would stay with me forever. "I understand."

"We'll see you when you get out."

Before she can walk away, I reach for her hand, which sends pain through my shoulder.

She seems taken aback, but clasps my cold palm, taking it in both of her hands.

"Promise me something."

"Sure," she responds, though with hesitancy in her eyes.

"Promise me you'll go on a date with me after this. Just one."

Kalen tries to cover her smirk, and coughs away a laugh.

I see a flash of sadness in Tessa's expression, but it is quickly gone. She takes a deep breath. "Okay. Just one date." She drops my hand and quietly exits the room.

Kalen lags behind. She gives me one last wave and an eye roll before disappearing as well.

In any other state, she would have probably said no. Seeing me like this softened her. These strange drugs are good for courage. They don't feel like the highs I'm used to, but they are still numbing, nonetheless.

I'm glad she said yes, but my mind can't help but wonder at the half-truths she and Kalen just gave me. Possibly lies.

Jessica's letter is still on my lap. I guess it is not the only mystery left in life.

Chapter Twenty-Six
Confessions of Love and Misery

"I do not fear losing you. I fear never to have had you in the first place."

~Edward McClage.

"Stop moving so much," Eliza commands. She stands a foot away, her fingers, for all intents and purposes, choking the life out of me.

"It'd probably be easier without that? You wouldn't have to reach so far." My eyes aim toward her belly, but all I can really see are the tops of her hands.

She pulls the tie harder. "Are you calling me fat?"

"Maybe I am."

She doesn't press further and instead puts more purpose into tying the awful contraption known as a tie. I used to make it a point not to wear ties at my events. Jessica always made a point to get me to. She always won.

"If I'd known this was part of the deal, I wouldn't have asked her."

Eliza cracks a smile. "Yes, you would have."

Definitely would have. I love her.

Eliza finally lets go, but I still feel like I'm choking. I reach for the knot, but she slaps my hand away. "You look good," she says. "Leave it."

I look in the mirror. I look ridiculous.

"Let me see," Roman says. He's standing in the doorway. I turn to the flash of a camera. He immediately holds up his hands. "Don't blame me. Mom wanted me to get a picture. Just making her happy."

Of course she did. I'm embarrassed by all of this. I feel like my high school prom all over again. I could use a solid hit right now. If only that was an option.

The sound of the doorbell saves me. Seeing Tessa will make all of this crap fade away. Not the most chivalrous of circumstances, having her pick me up, but I still don't have a license. Roman offered to call a cab, but that's even more embarrassing.

I hear Roman making his overly loud greeting.

I take a deep breath.

"You'll be fine," Eliza says. She cradles her belly as if it is her prize. I guess it really is. If anyone should know that, it's me. This Eliza is a far cry from the one that told me to take the job at the Art Studio. She seems less high strung. There's a peace in her eyes. I saw it in Jessica once. After she learned that she was pregnant.

Another breath, and I leave the room. It's been four days since I was discharged from the hospital, seven days since I killed Pete. It seems like a lifetime ago. It seems like a different life altogether. I killed someone. Now I'm going on a date.

But I still have the pain in my shoulder, and I scheduled my first counseling session two days from now. Also, a cop stopped by to ask me more questions. So, I guess it really is the same life. Maybe this is my third life. The first I lost my family. The second I lost my habit, I lost Montica, our child, and my only friend—my dealer. I wonder who, or what, I'll lose this time around. If this life lives up to the last two, it can only get worse.

Jessica would've hated my pessimism. But she would've loved the tie.

"Stop worrying," Eliza says, seemingly reading my cynical mind. If she only knew how much I've had taken from me, she probably wouldn't have the nerve to tell me that.

I see the back of Tessa first, her small frame hiding very little of Roman's hulking stature. Roman looks up when I come into the living room. He smiles and points my direction. "He cleans up quite well."

Tessa turns and her beautiful eyes meet mine. "He sure does," she agrees. She appears tired, maybe even agitated. I remember how she looked in the hospital. How she reacted when I asked her to go on this date. Maybe she is irritated. Irritated that I haven't given up yet. Irritated that she made the promise. Irritated that she is going out with a killer. Every time I think of Pete, I wonder what I'm doing now. How can I be doing this?

"You look beautiful." She's wearing a white dress with black stripes. It's form-fitting and displays how thin she really is.

"Thank you. Kalen picked it out. I would have probably dressed more like your mother had it been my way."

Roman awkwardly laughs and shuffles beside Eliza. "We'll leave you alone. Have a great time."

As soon as they're out of sight, Tessa's smile fades. "That wasn't fair asking me for this when you were in such a terrible state."

It takes me a moment to respond. "Well, would you have said yes any other time?"

Tessa shakes her head slowly. "No, I wouldn't have. I told you that I can't give you what you want."

"Why not?"

"I just can't."

I grab her hand. "All I want is a date." Her words hurt, but after the pain I've felt this past year, it's not near hurtful enough that I can't bear it. And I need to get my mind off of the memory of how a fork feels when it enters the jugular of another human being.

She grins a little. "That's all, really?"

"Yep, plain and simple."

"No confessions of love and misery?"

"None." I hope not. I really can't make any promises.

Tessa sighs. "Okay. I'm sure you have something else planned, but can we take a walk first?"

She's wrong. I have nothing planned, but I'm not going to let her know that. "If that's what you want, then that's fine with me."

Her body loses tension. She squeezes my hand and pulls me along.

It's a cool day for the first week of September. But Lafayette still shows signs of the summer. Scorched grass. The buzzing of air conditioners in an otherwise, quiet neighborhood. And very few people outside.

I follow Tessa as she pulls me along similar streets. We don't speak, but I'm content with having her hand in mine.

As the historic neighborhood melts away, and downtown Lafayette appears, familiar memories pour into my mind. Different memories, not dark ones. There's an old building where Roman and I got drunk the first time. Dad caught us. He grounded us for two months. As far as I know, Roman has never drank anything but the occasional glass of wine ever since.

When I got my first car, we raced each other down Columbia Street. Right by the police station. We got caught, but Officer Coast was a friend from church. He told us he wouldn't tell our parents if we promised to never do it again. We promised and then picked a better place to drag race outside of town.

College years took the youthful edge away from our lives. Roman went on to body-building and I moved on to art.

"We picked a good time to come. Not many kids," Tessa says, probably just to have something to say.

Columbian Park is somewhat empty now that school has started. The first time I met Tessa, we fought here. I told her I wanted to die. She told me I didn't. There was something intriguing about her, but I was too angry to accept it.

"Did you know Ritchie just started school?"

I didn't.

"Thanks to you," she adds.

"That money never should have been mine in the first place. How's he doing?"

"Excelling," she says. "I think being at the center was actually a hindrance. I think that happens sometimes. Like with Angela."

"The mute girl?"

Tessa is leading me back to our swings. "Not mute. And apparently, she said some words to you?"

I remember the small girl pointing at *Roger's World* and exclaiming how beautiful it was. Her staff said it had been years since they'd heard any other words uttered from her mouth. That's hard to believe, but I've seen crazier things lately. I've been the crazier thing.

Tessa grabs her swing and falls into it. "It's a little different from that first night we met, huh?"

"A little," I say, sitting down on the swing beside her.

"Why do you think that is?"

"You."

Tessa turns away from me, but not before I can see the red on her cheeks. "Why do you continue to do that? I told you, I can't."

I've heard her loud and clear every time, but I have yet to hear a reason why. She's not telling me something. I know, because I followed up on her claims at the hospital. She has no client named Jamie Bridges. She lied to me. She wasn't visiting anyone. There's more to her life that she's not sharing with me.

I start to speak, but she interrupts me. "No confessions of love or misery. That was my condition."

I don't care. "Screw your conditions, Tessa. I lost my wife less than a year ago. I lost the child inside of her. I lost Montica and the life we made together. I lost myself, numbing anything and everything I could possibly feel. Without you, I would be dead. You were right that night. I didn't want to die. I wanted to live. I want to live now. With you. Stop lying to me and tell me why we can't be together! Give me a reason and I'll understand. I've been through so much worse. You can't hurt me anymore than I already have been before." I hope that last statement is true.

Tessa is stone-faced during my proclamation. After a moment of silence, she exhales loudly. She blinks and the tears appear. "You just don't understand. I told you just a date. You're breaking your promise."

"I don't care. You saved me. I love you."

The tears start streaming down her face, and glisten off her pale skin. "You promised."

Even though she's crying, I can't help but laugh at her view of me. "I'm not a good person. Why do you expect more of me?" I just killed a man. I'm as bad as they come.

She continues to sob. "I don't know."

I leave the swing and kneel down before her, clutching her hands. "You bared your soul to me. Told me your past. About your family. The abuse. About Kalen. Why can't you be honest with me now?"

"I just can't."

"You're the only person in the world who knows the truth about what I've lost. About the children I'll never know. The true extent of my suffering. I've told you everything. All I'm asking is that you tell me why you don't love me back? I know there's a million reasons why you shouldn't, but you haven't told me even one of them. And I need to hear it from your lips."

No response.

"Just give me something Tessa. Look at me. I gave up all semblance of life because I lost everything that I ever loved before. Doesn't that show you who I am. Jessica had every part of me. When she died, she took it all with her. Now, I feel like I have something again, and I'm willing to give it all to you. Doesn't that mean something?"

She wipes the tears from her eyes and clears her throat. "It does. Wes, I see your life and it reminds me of my own. The pain, the suffering. The desire to drown in self-made misery. But I found faith in God. I found friends that became family. Not one person to grasp on to. I'm afraid you are just trying to replace your self-made misery with some infatuation."

Can God just get out of the picture? Her words make sense from her point of view, but she can't really see inside of my heart. How I truly feel.

"I can't let you do that. I won't let you."

There's no real weight behind what should be very resolute words. She seems sheepish, half-truths to hide what is really going on.

I need to know the truth, so I change my approach. If she doesn't want my confessions of love and misery, then she gets an inquisition. "You weren't visiting someone at the hospital. I know that."

Her eyes immediately betray her. She tries to look away, but I've already seen the reaction.

"And during the project, you kept missing days. The staff said you were going to appointments. And you look different."

Tessa stands up. "No. I have to go."

I grab her arm.

"Let go of me!" she yells.

"Please, just tell me what is going on!" I plead with her. I have to know.

She jerks hard, but it feels weak. She's weak.

"Are you sick?"

Tessa begins to sob again, but she doesn't fight any more.

I stand and embrace her, feeling my own tears forming. Something inside tells me I don't want her to answer my questions anymore, but I can't go on without knowing the truth. Why can't she love me?

"Are you sick?" I ask again.

Tessa takes a step away from me.

I feel my world crashing down with the weight of her eyes.

She looks uneasy, maybe dizzy.

"I'm not sick," she says, stumbling back another step. "I'm dying. I'm dying, Wes."

My mind registers the words. My heart stops beating. But I don't have time to allow the feelings to take over. Tessa stumbles forward. I catch her, and slowly lower her to the ground. She's lifeless in my arms. Lifeless as Pete was on the pavement of 14th Street.

I panic and scream.

Chapter Twenty-Seven
The Truth of Things Two

It's my second ambulance ride in less than two weeks. I'm incoherent for both. I stare aimlessly at the ambulance sidewall, as Tessa lies on the stretcher before me. I hear things like "she's breathing," and "she's stable," but there's only two words that stick in my mind.

I'm dying.

Deep down, I knew something was wrong. From the moment Kalen betrayed some unknown emotion, an expression contrary to her usual disposition, something in my mind clicked. She was vulnerable that morning we had breakfast together. It was a brief moment, but so much was said in her eyes. Her actions.

And I knew it was true.

But I needed Tessa to say the words so my mind could accept what my heart was already telling me. Things were too good to be true.

I'm ushered into the hospital, following a parade of busy bodies huddled around her. She is yet another one of God's unfair thefts. Of all the people, and He's taking her? He could have taken me a year ago. He could have saved me from the Hell I've lived. From the Hell I'm still living now.

Tessa brought me out of this darkness. Now, she'll be the one that throws me back in it. Well, her God will be. If everything she tells me is true, if everything Roman believes is factual, if the faith that Jessica had before she died is real, then God hates me more than anyone in the world. Do I deserve this? How can one man be expected to lose so much and survive it? I'm wicked, I know, but this is just too much to bear—for anyone.

Sunday after Sunday I went to church. I prayed to Him. I sang His praises. Night after night, Jessica talked about this God. She lived and breathed Him, just like my family. All the things my parents taught us. Those lessons stuck with Roman, but I've never been able to stomach them. I played the part for Jessica, doing just enough to keep her love. But I never gave in to the sentiment that God cared for me. And this is just proof that it's true. It's always been true. I believe He exists. This burden is just too much to be coincidental. I'm paying for something, though I have no idea for what.

And apparently, I'll continue paying for it for the rest of my life. I thought killing Pete was finally it, the lowest I could go. But this will be the catalyst to take me lower.

I'm not sure how I reach the waiting area. My mind suspects that someone led me here, but I don't remember a thing.

I'm numb to sound. Numb to feeling. Numb to everything but the simple facts. The room is white. The chairs are beige. There's a family that keeps walking by, dad and two daughters. I've counted four nurses walking down the adjacent hall. Some back and forth several times. Hospital noises. The same ones I heard earlier this week when I was stuck in a hospital bed of my own, one floor up.

Now it's Tessa, somewhere in this building, apparently dying. Of what? Why didn't she tell me? I fell in love with her, opened my entire heart and soul to her, but she couldn't tell me the truth. I guess that's the answer I was looking for. Why we couldn't be together.

I don't know how long I've been sitting here. It could have been five minutes or five hours. It's all the same.

"I'm sorry."

I pick up my head to see Joseph leaning against the wall. Kalen stands beside him, her face showing no emotion.

"You knew?" I ask.

"Yes, it's not uncommon knowledge," Joseph answers. "She's stable for now. And awake."

"Why didn't anyone tell me?"

Joseph sits down beside me. Kalen remains standing. "It wasn't for us to tell."

"Everyone knows because of Mom's work," Kalen adds. "And her different connections to several organizations. It's been a long battle, so no one really thinks of it as a secret. Everyone just knows. And Mom isn't real keen on bringing it up." Kalen bites her lip. "For my sake."

"So, she really is dying?"

Kalen nods. "Yes."

Hearing it from someone else's mouth makes it even more real. I feel fresh tears forming behind my eyelids. "From what?"

"She has HIV. From the years of drugs and shared needles. It's weakened her immune system, allowing the cancer in her lymph nodes to spread. The lymphoma is deadly. Chemo didn't work. The other treatments didn't work. But for the most part, she's been okay, until the last few months. She's digressing rapidly." Kalen says the words as if she's rehearsed them a million times.

The world is too cruel. God is too cruel. She should have been done suffering from cruelty. Yet its grip on her has never left. It's held onto her until there is no life left to take. All she does is give, and yet everything is being taken away.

The question is painful to ask, because I don't really want to know the answer. But the words slip out between my lips before I can stop them. "How long?"

"A couple of weeks. Maybe a month," Kalen responds. For the first time, I see a hint of despair in her eyes, followed by the obvious glint of tears. "But they've been giving her this answer for the last year or so. I guess God's not ready to take her yet." Kalen takes a seat and turns away from me. She continues. "Every day I think it could be her last. Every time she leaves I wonder if I will ever see her alive again."

Joseph places his hand on her shoulder, the fatherly figure that he is. He's seen heartache just as I have. He's been where she is.

"It's a life that I wouldn't wish on anyone," Kalen continues, her voice cracking under the sorrow.

My heart sinks with every word. After a few moments, her voice trails away into some distant whisper and my mind conjures up a devastating memory.

It was Autumn when she died. But I remember it being very hot the day we laid her to rest. I remember thinking how cold the dirt must feel on such a humid day. I remember thinking about anything other than what was actually happening before me.

I was already drunk, a product of the wine that Jessica kept on hand for long days on the job. For several days after her death, I was numb, but slowly the realization of my wife and my child being gone bore down on me, and I didn't know how to escape it. So, I drank. And I thought about killing myself, but I was too weak to follow through. The night of the funeral I lay in the guest bathtub, razor blade in hand. For twelve hours I held that blade next to my left wrist, contemplating how it would feel to run that sharpened edge down my forearm. Contemplating how it would feel to die slowly. It would be nothing like her death. But what did it matter? I'd see her again, I'd hoped.

The next morning when the first light came through the bathroom window, I threw the blade as hard as I could. It stuck in the wall right behind the sink. As far as I know, it's still there. I could not take the pain away, and I could not take my own life. So, I turned to something else. I found Pete. And he gave me exactly what I wanted. He gave me what I needed to be numb from the pain. To be numb from the realization of what my life had become. What it would be like without her. The drugs were much better than Jessica's "long day" wine.

The reclusive lifestyle, the sex, the general disdain for life was just a side-effect of the prescription. I became addicted because it meant I could hide away from it all.

Now that feeling is coming back.

I have no reason to live. And I need a way to numb myself from this.

"Hi, are you Kalen?" The doctor's words bring me back to the present.

Kalen nods slowly, her face shows both fear and the resolve to face it. Where does she get that from? I suppose from Tessa.

I see Roman and Eliza coming down the hall behind the doctor. Roman looks like he is trying to slow her down, but Eliza has that motherly look on her face. She's looking directly at me.

"You can visit her now, but I must let you know, she's one or two more of these bouts from being gone. A few weeks," the doctor says. He's an older gentleman. Looks like a lifetime of stress has had its way with him.

Kalen nods again.

I, on the other hand, can't comprehend his words, even if they have been said before. *A few weeks and she'll be gone.* I stand just as Roman grabs my arm. I pull away. "I've got to go. I can't take this."

Kalen turns toward me. "She needs you."

"Don't go," Eliza pleads. "Don't run away from us again."

There's an underlying anger that surfaces. They all knew, and I didn't. "No, I can't do this. I can't go through this again."

"Please!" Kalen cries.

"Please don't go back." Eliza starts to cry.

As I run, I imagine her falling into Roman's arms. I imagine Joseph embracing Kalen, and all of them just standing there watching me flee.

I run. From them. From the truth. From everything, hoping that I can once again hide behind my present god, and this time never come back to the real world.

Chapter Twenty-Eight
In Memoriam

If I don't overdose tonight, then nothing will kill me. I have enough drugs for an entire gang. Enough alcohol to drown a drunk. And no sense of modesty or inhibition to hinder me. Pete's gone, but I don't need him.

I was too old for this club when Montica brought me here. I'm too old now, but I don't draw any attention. I'm a washed-up artist. These kids don't know who I am. They don't care. I could be a rapist, a murderer, but as long as I keep the alcohol flowing, free of their dime, I'm king.

It's been over a month since I've had any drugs, since I've fallen into their grasp, but it's just so natural... so familiar. The mindless ecstasy, the blackouts, the unnatural length of the night, and most importantly, the numbness from all of reality. I fall into it so easily. Like an old friend, I revel in it.

Hip hop beats blare through the speakers, pounding so obnoxiously loud that the sounds almost feel like they are a part of the scenery, an extension of my physical surroundings. I feel like I can see the waves around me, feel them inside of me. The thud of the bass becomes my heartbeat.

It would've been beyond Jessica to see me in a place like this.

But I'm not thinking of her. Another drink, another hit.

The sea of faces comes and goes, some familiar, some new. After a while, I lose track of the distinctions. It's just a blurry sea of figures. Voices call out to me. "More drinks." I oblige. What little money I have saved is gone. I have no credit. The card I gave away is locked. It won't be long before the bank runs dry, and the till comes calling.

"Cheers!" a young girl yells, splashing her beer on me.

She looks like Montica. I cringe and look away.

I can't think of her. Another drink, another hit.

Broad shoulders come toward me. I ignore them and sway with some rhythmic dance song. It reeks of youth and excess.

A hand grabs my shoulder. I pull away and try to take a step. Another hand, more firm this time. I hear a burly voice, but it's too low to make out. But it's authoritative, not wild and carefree like the friends I've made.

The funds are gone, and I'm still offering drinks on my tab. The staff have caught on. I try to pull away again, but another set of hands grabs my waist. I turn and swing as hard as I can. I don't know why. I'm not mad or upset. I'm just not ready to leave.

I feel the pressure of a large fist hit my jaw. Teeth rattle, I see black momentarily. I wake with another swing. I clearly miss, and two forceful hands push me to the ground.

"Take it easy," one of the black-shirted men says. "Don't make this hard, dude."

I struggle, but I'm in no fashion to fight. "Carry me out of here then you large freaks!" I yell over the music.

One of the men laughs. "No problem."

The crowd boos as I'm walked across the dance floor. No more alcohol on me. The rich guy at the club is no more. If only they knew how little I actually had. They drank away all that I had left.

The freaks don't take any time setting me down. I hit the sidewalk hard. The door closes seconds later, and the dubstep beats die. The city of Lafayette greets me with a deathly quiet, middle-of-Indiana calm.

I'm alone, no money, and nowhere to go. I can't see any familiar faces. They would only remind me of her. It's too late. I think of Tessa. I need another drink, another hit. But unfortunately, this time I have access to neither.

Although I've thought about it, I've never actually said as much directly to Him. So, I look up to the sky and laugh. "God, you win. You might as well just kill me now. What more can you do?"

Distant thunder. Maybe that's His answer.

I look to the west just in time to see a flash of lightning. Under the flash I see the road wind up to the other Twin City. I see Purdue buildings, the college basically its own village within West Lafayette. The last time I was over the river was when Montica devastated me. But I've not been up that far past the river in some time. Not where the thunder is coming from. About a year.

And there's only one reason for that. That's where she is now. I've never visited her. I could never find the strength to.

But tonight, I'm on empty. She's all I have left.

I slip in and out of Roman and Eliza's without detection, despite them being home.

Letter in hand, I set out for West Lafayette, on my way to a certain plot of land on the north side of the commercial district. Tippecanoe Memory Gardens.

It took me about an hour to walk here. It was quiet, and though my brain is buzzed with narcotics, I feel rather clear-headed in my thoughts. I don't feel a strong urge to run away or hide from the truth. Jessica is buried here, and I've been too wrapped up in my own guilt and self-pity to come back. I watched her get lowered into the ground, and it's a haunting memory, but I can't even remember what part of the cemetery she's in, or what's written on her stone.

Small memory cues lead me in a general direction. A dirt path that I remember, only because my head was down most of that day. I was too afraid to look up. Black shoes on dry dirt. There's a small building, where I assume garden tools and other miscellaneous cemetery items reside. I remember seeing Roman's large frame standing before it in one of the few glances I allowed myself during the small service.

I continue to walk on the path and around the building, forming a picture of where I was in relation to it. Before I can distinguish the exact vantage point, I see a large marble stone, rounded on the top. It doesn't bring back any vivid memory or light bulb moment, but I know immediately it's hers.

My world stops for a moment. I feel a rush of pain in my chest. A pain that I've for so long tried to conceal.

My knees hit the dirt, directly in front of the ornate stone.

Jessica Lynn Gerhard.
March 27th, 1990 to November 27th, 2015.

"I'm sorry it took so long," I whisper, barely able to form words.

It starts to rain. I notice enough to put her letter in my shirt. I'm not strong enough to open it anyway. Who am I kidding?

"I'm so sorry."

I halfway expect there to be a response. But that girl that stood on the beach, the one whose memories are single-handedly the best part of my life, is as gone as she was that moment her car flipped over and the impact took her and my child to some other realm. For her sake, I hope that the Heaven she believed in is real.

Of course, the way I'm living, that's no relief to me.

I know I wouldn't deserve to see her again, anyway. The rain comes down harder, and I bow to the weight collecting in the fabric of my clothes. My knees sink into the mud, and a cold chill surges through me.

Here I am in a prostrate position, bowing before the god of my life. The person I can't let go. I don't want to let go. And yet, she gives me no answers.

But then I see the words inscribed beneath her dates, a phrase so familiar it's like seeing an old friend.

'Oh to see the face of God! I feel Him within this place. I hear Him. I see His work within this great city. One night in London is all I need.' Edward McClage

Tessa's words—Jessica's words—right in front of me. One night in London. That's all Tessa wanted. My heart breaks in half with the thought that maybe this is Jessica's answer. Maybe even in death she knows more than I do. Maybe London was never that place across the ocean. Maybe this God was all she was ever seeking. And maybe this hell of a situation was orchestrated by the man upstairs Himself.

It's no consolation.

For the second time tonight, I cry out to this unseen being. "Why? Can't there be another way? Why do you have to take everything away from me? Just answer me."

I stare up at the sky, allowing the rain to cover my tears. It comes down harder, but I don't move.

Hours pass by in darkness, just enough light from a nearby lamp to cast my shadow over her dimly lit gravestone. The rain continues, soaking me to the bone. I shiver. I falter. But I continue to wait.

No answers ever come.

Slowly the night starts to hide its face, and a glow decides to show itself over the horizon, the sun making its first appearance. Finally, the rain stops. Still cold and wet, but I refuse to move. I retrieve her letter. Maybe the answers I seek are inside this piece of parchment. The last secret she holds.

There's one problem. I couldn't open it five or six hours ago, and I can't open it now. It's been nearly a year, but her final words will still remain hidden from me.

I'm hungover and defeated.

I'm not sure how many hours of daylight pass before I hear the sign of visitors, but the crunching of rocks under tires stirs me from my waking slumber. I listen to the telltale signs of a loved one coming to visit their lost family member or friend, but I don't look. I don't have the will to move.

Abruptly, the car noises stop, replaced by light footfalls. This new sound moves closer to me until I can sense that I'm the one being visited.

I don't need to look up to know who it is. I just know. "How did you know I was here?"

"Lucky guess," Kalen softly responds.

"No one is that lucky." I feel her standing next to me.

"We looked everywhere else."

I look up at her face, expecting to see tears and sleepiness. Instead, I see strong resolve. "Who's we?"

"Joseph. You know, he cares about you deeply."

I allow a chuckle beneath my breath. "Everyone seems to care about me deeply. I've given them no reason to care. I've given you no reason to spend your night searching for me. You should be with your mom."

Kalen falls to a seat in the wet grass beside me. She grins. "Most people would say that, but I think—and I know she does too—that you need me more than she does right now."

How can she say that? All of my strength is gone, but there are still tears available. I melt onto Kalen's lap and cry some more. She doesn't move.

I don't know how long I'm in this position, but eventually, Kalen places her hand across my back. "I can't even count how many times I've cried like this? Too many,

Mom says. I know you've seen a lot of crap, but can you imagine watching your mother slowly die before you? And half the time, she doesn't even show it because she's too busy caring about other people."

I can't imagine it. I lost Jessica so quickly, but to know of her demise for months, even years. It would've destroyed me even more, if that's possible.

"I've resented you people for so long. But I finally just gave up." Kalen sighs. "Why even try, when she's happy. Who am I to judge her for doing what she thinks is right? That's when I stopped crying for her. When I realized that helping people like you is what makes what little life she has left worth living."

Kalen sounds years older than she is. Her life has forced her to grow up beyond her age. But even with everything I've been through, I could never have come to the place she is at. She's better than me. Far better.

"Did your mother tell you to come find me?"

"No," Kalen answers, and I can sense her smiling and shaking her head. "It was my idea."

I pull my drenched frame away from her and wipe the wetness from my eyes. "Why?" I look at her, dressed like some goth punk from a metal band, but I don't see the stereotype. I see a small version of Tessa. Of Jessica. And it pains me.

"Because, I figured out that if I want to be happy like my mother, then I have to do the things that make her happy. I have to live my life like she does, follow her example." Kalen pauses for a second. I can see the thoughts processing in her mind. Her focus returns to me and she exhales before continuing. "I know you won't want to hear this, but I think it's what needs to be said."

God will be coming back into this conversation.

"But hear me out. The reason my mom can be happy is that she's not living for herself. She's living for things outside of her. Outside of her condition. She's living for God, she's living for others. Right now, you only think about yourself, and that's why you can't understand why she can be happy in this."

Being reprimanded by a teenage girl should sting more. But she's right.

"Clearly, I never met your wife, but from what I've heard, she was a lot like Mom."

"She was your mom through and through," I respond. I remember times where I saw Jessica standing in front of me where Tessa once was. "That's why I fell in lov—" I choke on the word.

"I know," Kalen quickly responds. "I know you love her. And she loves you. And I'm sure your wife loved you dearly, but I'm pretty certain Jessica would not have been drunk sitting beside your tombstone had you died. I'm pretty sure she wouldn't have lived how you are living now. Have you ever thought what she would have done if it was the other way around?"

Never. Not once. But now that my mind is thinking of it, I know Kalen is one hundred percent correct. Jessica would have been hurt deeply, but never would she have done this. I've lost so much, but even if it was possible for her to have lost me and our child, she would've pulled through. She cared too little about her own gain and too much for others to let death defeat her. She was too strong for that. Just like Tessa, death is too little of a thing to allow victory to it.

Because they believe in someone far greater. They believe in a supreme being and an afterlife with Him. My whole family does. That's why they are stronger.

I know Him too, but not like they do. And I'm still too angry for what He's taken to change that.

But, there are things I can change. "I'm sorry. I should be there for her."

Kalen grins. "Why don't you tell her that?"

I clutch Jessica's letter. I don't have to read it to understand what the answers are. It will have to wait for another day.

I look back at her grave. "She was amazing. No person could deserve her."

"That's how I feel about Mom. But no one deserves what we've been given. We've been given more than most. You didn't deserve the perfect wife. I don't deserve the perfect mom. So, we shouldn't expect to keep them forever."

No, we shouldn't. But everything in me does. That's why I'm fundamentally different from Jessica and Tessa, and even Kalen.

I read the words on Jessica's gravestone again. They personify her life. Even McClage knew things that I don't, as much as I hate to admit it.

"Can we go now? Joseph promised not to leave."

For the first time tonight, I see how pitiful I am. Soaked and drunk. This is the person that everyone is trying to save. And they are happy to do it. I'm starting to understand this theory of happiness. I don't like it. And I don't think I'll ever reach the plateau that these people in my life have reached.

But I can try.

Chapter Twenty-Nine
Theory of Happiness

If I had only one wish—and the divine genie refused to bring back a loved one—then I would ask for this: one more day with her. Just one more day to hold Jessica in my arms and tell her how much I love her. To thank her for everything that she gave to me. Just one more day to bask in the mystery of her selfless love. One more day. Just one.

Most of the time I'd feel sorry for myself, then hide away in a bottle or some pills. But today I've been gifted with another opportunity. No, it's not one more day with my wife. I'll never get her back. That's just a fact of this hellish reality we call life.

But Kalen showed me that I've been given another chance with Tessa. What I didn't have with my wife, I now have with this woman who's forced her way into my present reality. If only for a short time. But the impact is deeper than I think she'll ever know.

All I can give Tessa is a date. By her request this time.

"Out of all the places, and this is where you wanted to go?"

Tessa kicks her legs in and out, forcing the swing to move faster. The signs of her illness are present, the dark circles under her eyes, her thinning stature, all symptoms I'd noticed before, but nothing that would indicate her life is nearing its end. I try to force that thought from my mind.

"It's where everything started. That night you told me you wanted to die."

"I lied."

She grins. "I know. I'm glad."

I slouch in my own swing, staring out at the emptiness of Columbian Park at 5 a.m. That night I thought I knew how I felt about the life I was barely living. That was before I fell in love with her. Before I had something new to live for. As much as I want to believe the fairytale will have a happy ending, I know it won't.

"You know, when I met you that night, I saw so much of myself. When I first got the diagnosis, I wanted to go back to that place where drugs ruled me, where I could drown. You described exactly how I felt. And I knew I had to be a part of your life."

In some ways, I wish I'd never seen her again. Then I wouldn't have to feel this nagging pain inside of me. Of course, that would involve her not forcing herself into my life. The other part of me can't stand the thought of her not being here, now. Not feeling so drawn to her. "That's what you do, you help people. I don't know how or why you live this way. How you'll die this way, but you seem happy."

Tessa pushes her feet in the ground, slowing the black swing to a stop. She reaches into her back pocket, pulling out her phone and a small photo. "I keep this with me wherever I go," she says, extending the small rectangular object toward me.

I take it and flip it over. There's just enough light from a nearby pole to make out the picture. It's of a small girl on a swing. I recognize a much younger Kalen.

"That photo was taken when I didn't have custody of her. I know Kalen came to you. And I know she acts as though my self-sacrificial life is foreign to her, but it's all because of her. God used her to make me who I am. She saved me when I was a drug addict. She saved me when I wanted to lie in bed until I died. She saved me from dying without seeing you again." Tessa puts her hands on mine. "Am I right?"

I nod. "If she wouldn't have come to find me, I probably would have hidden away in my numb state until you were long gone."

"She's stronger than I'll ever be."

What Tessa doesn't understand is that Kalen is her. A younger version of herself. A younger version of Jessica. They are all the same. They are what I have never been able to be.

I place the photo back into her hands before clutching them in my own. "I love you, Tessa. I would give anything for us to be together for the rest of our lives."

She smiles. A single tear rolls down her left cheek. "I know." The last time I told her this—in this very spot—I found out she was dying. Three nights ago, what feels like a lifetime. But this time, she doesn't turn away from me, and she doesn't cringe at my words. Instead, her grip tightens around my fingers. "I love you, too. I tried to hide it so you wouldn't feel this hurt again. First with your wife, then with Montica." Her grip grows stronger, but her smile softens. "But it's not the love you are looking for. I'm sorry, but I just don't have that to give."

I should feel a great sense of despair hearing this confession. She doesn't love me the way that I love her, and she will die that way.

But, contrary to myself, I'm okay. I think I understand. I'd given everything to Jessica, and when she died, she took it all with her. Well, I thought she did. But I found love again. But Tessa's given everything to everyone else, so how can I expect her to have anything left to give at the end.

"I really am sorry."

"There's no need to be." I fake a smile. "I think I get it."

Her smile returns, then something catches her attention. She turns to the east, where a long row of trees extends down the sidewalk, a street lined with parking spots on the other side, and houses beyond that. I can see the first sign of light coming between two old white houses.

"That's what this date is all about," she proclaims. "One more sunrise."

The resoluteness in her voice, mixed with the concrete understanding that this could very well be the last sunrise she'll ever witness, tears a hole inside of me. I can't contain my own tears. I want to wipe them away, but she holds my hands firmly in place.

Together, we watch as the sun slowly ascends, and life begins for the bustling metropolis of Lafayette. Birds chirp, traffic grows, and darkness fades. It's not some ocean view, or a portrait landscape, but watching the sun rise over the houses and the trees—with her—is more than enough for me.

I know that this moment will be one of *those* moments I'll hold on to for the rest of my life. I'll hate this memory and cherish it at the same time, knowing that I'll never have another piece of time like this one, while remembering that this moment will allow me to keep a little piece of her with me forever. Just like the memory of Jessica on the beach. Other things will pass. This won't.

It's starting to get hot when Tessa stirs. The sun's now high above us. She releases my grasp. "Thank you," she whispers.

"I should be thanking you."

She ignores my comment by standing and stretching. "How do you feel?"

"Fine." I should be asking her that question.

After a couple more stretches and an overly dramatic yawn, she reaches for my hand again. I offer, and she pulls me out of the swing. "I have one other place to take you tonight—I mean, today. I know, it's a long date."

I'd spend the rest of my life on this date if I could. "Let's go."

She leads me away from the park and past the familiar streets. Just past the old hospital where new construction has started.

We walk down 26th street, quietly. There's so much I want to say, but don't even know where to start. I resign myself to just being with her. Knowing that it could be my last time. I'll have to live every moment as if it could be the last.

When we turn down Cason Street, there's no denying where we're headed. I can see the A.W.A. Resource Center in the distance. My art piece, *Roger's World*, stands out, an oddity among the row of dull brick buildings.

Tessa breaks the silence as we approach the center. "You know, the night you came over for dinner, the night we met, was all a sham."

I stop, waiting for more explanation.

She faces me, then pulls me into the lawn in front of my piece. "We knew you had taken the job. It wasn't just a coincidence."

I can't help but laugh at the idea. "You really think I'm that stupid. Roman and Eliza are smart. I figured as much."

She grins. "Good, I just didn't want to leave you with a lie."

Once again, worried about me when she should be worried about what little life she has left.

"Why here?" I look at *Roger's World* and I see Ritchie working like a dog, holding pieces of pipe up against the side of the building. I see Montica holding her notepad, writing down every crazed detail of my plan. I see myself, finding my passion again.

Tessa stares at the piece for a moment, then sighs. "Can I tell you another secret? One that I've had buried deep inside for a long time?"

I'm intrigued, but part of me knows these things come with the reality of a clear demise.

I nod.

She sighs again. "I hope this helps you in some way, but I just want to tell you a little more about my uncle."

I feel bile in my throat at the thought of him. The man who raped her and got away with it. The man who ruined a good portion of her life.

She must notice my disgust, but she doesn't show it. "Can I tell you?"

I nod again.

Tessa grabs my hand and pulls me to a seat in the grass. She situates herself directly in front of me, *Roger's World* looming behind her. I would be lying if I said that I'm not proud of the beautiful piece that Ritchie and I created. But superimposed before it, Tessa makes the piece look like a two-year-old's art project.

Right now, Tessa is that one night in London for me.

She takes a few deep breaths before starting. "The first time my uncle touched me, I cried that whole night. I was so ashamed, and I felt disgusting. So small. Insignificant. I didn't say anything because I couldn't. How does a young girl explain such vile things? And perhaps, I thought, it was the only time it would happen.

"I was wrong though. He continued. He'd make excuses to come over, or he would need a place to stay for the night. At first, he just touched me, then he forced me to sleep with him."

This is the last thing I wanted to hear today. But who am I to tell her what she can or can't talk about? All I can do is listen.

"For three years this continued. There were so many times that I wanted to tell my parents, but every time I tried, I couldn't. I don't know why, but I just couldn't do it.

Thank God, I finally got pregnant. That was what it took. My mother was with me at the doctor's office when they told me.

"And then I let everything out. The nurse was horrified, my mother looked as if she was going to die right there. She couldn't believe that her brother-in-law would do this. She didn't believe. Neither of my parents did. My dad loved his brother dearly. Took care of him his whole life. They just couldn't grasp it. Not until the blood tests proved it was his. And my uncle never denied it. He didn't care."

"And they still refused to believe by wanting you to put her up for adoption?"

Tessa nods. "I've not spoken with them since. And they wouldn't even pursue charges. They didn't want my uncle to go to jail. They bribed me to keep quiet."

This part of the story doesn't make sense. "Wait. I thought you said he was in prison."

Tessa looks at me sheepishly, then turns toward *Roger's World*. "You're right, I did tell you that. I lied."

I feel a distinct burning in my chest, a wrath that supersedes all other emotions. It mirrors what I felt when I saw the bruises on Ritchie, but it's stronger. How could this man be free?

"I know what you're thinking," Tessa replies, still facing away from me. "You want justice. As did I."

"I want him dead."

She turns back to me. "Well, in some senses your wish was granted. My uncle was always a dangerous man. That's why it wasn't strange when I found out he had crashed his Maserati going a hundred miles an hour down an Arizona highway."

I feel some sense of relief. "So, he is dead."

Tessa shakes her head. "No, like I said, in a sense. He suffered a traumatic brain injury that left him a different person. He lost his entire identity and became a kind-hearted, giving eight-year-old in a fifty-year-old's body. The evil man was gone."

"How do you know all of this if you haven't talked to your parents?"

"They've left messages, letters. But I've never responded. Even if my heart has forgiven them, I don't feel the need to pursue the relationship we once had. But that doesn't matter. I learned all of this from them. His brain was forever altered."

I feel no sympathy. In fact, I'm disgusted by her story. I want him gone. For good. I don't care what he became. And I don't like where this story is going. She forgave her parents? Now, she works with people just like him. Is this why she works in this field? Is she torturing herself?

She reaches for my hand and locks her fingers in mine. "I find it justice. His former life was dismissed, and he lived a selfless, childlike existence. He gave his all to other people. He was a good man. The opposite of what he once was. The things he once hated, he grew to love. And at his funeral, to which my parents did not attend, he was celebrated for a life that gave so much more than he ever took. That's justice enough for me."

I pull away from her. "You can't say that. He was a monster, no matter what happened to him."

She extends her hand again, waiting for me to take it. I do.

"Are you telling me you forgive him?"

She nods. "His life changed. He served others just like I've tried to do."

I can't stomach it, but I don't offer any more rebuttals. "What happened to him?"

Tessa grips my hand tighter. "He used the rest of his life to build up others. To inspire a community. To die a hero."

The relief comes back. He is dead.

"Then, he died last year." She turns toward the piece again. "He made such an impact that they decided to make a memorial for him."

I look at *Roger's World* and nearly throw up. She can't be talking about this piece—my piece. She can't be.

"My uncle's name was Roger Perretti. He was a hero to the city of Lafayette. He did more for this community than most people will ever know. And I came here six months ago to be a part of it." When she turns back toward me, her eyes are filled with tears. "I came here to be a part of this change, even if it was only for his last few weeks of life. God took away the evil man that took my childhood, and replaced him with a man that only wanted to do what was best for others. A man that found Jesus, believed in His sacrifice, and lived a life for God. I had nothing to do with that. That was God's justice. But I found a way to forgive, and a way to embrace God's plan for what little life I have left. I was a part of Roger's world, just as I am a part of yours. God used Roger to make me who I am, just like He used Kalen. And I believe He's using my short time on this earth to help you become who you need to be."

"No!" I yell. "I can't listen to this." I pull away again. Nothing about this is right. She can't forgive him. She just can't. "How can you live like this?"

Tessa's hands find my shoulders. "Why is this so hard for you to believe? I decided to live what life I had without bitterness. Without sorrow and shame. I decided to live. And I needed to forgive him. To see what he had become first hand and accept it. Because God forgave me."

I shrug her hands away. "He was a monster!"

Tessa grabs me again, pulling me toward her so that we are face to face. "So are you!"

I choke back any words I had.

"He *was* a monster. He took my innocence. You did the same to Montica. She looked up to you, and you stole from her. But I chose to forgive him because I felt I had to if I ever wanted to find peace."

Her words are a dagger. I want to fight back, but I can't. She's right. I took what wasn't mine. I ruined Montica's life before it even started. I put a life inside of her. A life that died. And now, she's gone.

I want to scream, but I can't. "You're right," I concede. "But I've never been forgiven. I took her life and now I have to live with it. That's my burden. It should forever be my burden. I don't deserve her forgiveness. And neither does he."

Tessa's abruptly harsh façade fades away. A thin smile comes over her lips. "That's where you're wrong. And don't be so sure. Montica adores you."

Adores. Present tense. "You've spoken with her?"

Tessa smiles broadly now, which conveys her answer. "You've had a terrible life this past year. You've lost so much, and you've destroyed your life on your own. You've become a monster, but that doesn't mean you can't change. That doesn't mean that there isn't forgiveness. There is. God took Roger's life and shaped him into something that was the antithesis of who he once was. It's not fair, not what we would think right, but that doesn't matter. You have the chance to make a change on your own. Don't let a crash be the catalyst. You still have a chance. A choice."

I don't know how that is true. But I can't argue with her conviction. She has been right about everything. Every part of me. I have changed. I've fallen, but I'm here now, sober. How can I question her? I can't yet resolve the fact that the Roger that stole her innocence is the same Roger I created a piece for. The same Roger that the community fell in love with. I can't, and I won't reconcile it. She's right, it isn't fair. It isn't right.

But none of that matters because I can't fight against her anymore.

I do what only I can do. The only thing that I have left to do. I believe her. Someday, maybe I can be forgiven. That doesn't mean I can understand how she allowed herself to come to terms with this form of justice that only God can give. My piece will now forever be tainted. I'm not sure I'll ever be able to look at *Roger's World* in the same way. But that doesn't matter. I take this surprise twist in Tessa's long life of sacrifice and file it away.

I must separate the two Roger's if I'm ever able to understand how I can find forgiveness, or hope, or any semblance of change.

"You really think there is hope for me, don't you?"

"Yes, I do."

I embrace Tessa as if it's the last time. "I'm so happy Roman and Eliza brought you to me."

She pushes herself away, holding me at arm's length. "They didn't."

I'm not sure my mind understands what she's saying. "What?"

"You said that they brought me to you. They didn't."

I heard correctly, but I have no idea what she's talking about. "I'm confused. What do you mean?"

Tessa's beautiful green eyes look so deeply into mine that I fear looking away. There's a world in there that I have yet to discover. That I will never discover. There are so many layers left untouched. After a moment, she pulls me back into her grasp. I feel her breath on my skin as she whispers into my ear. "They never came to me. I came to them."

Her declaration should leave me breathless. It should shock me, make me question everything. But Kalen's words come back so clearly. *Mom's always trying to help someone.*

Of course she did. Leave it to Tessa to search out a worthless man like me and try to do something about it.

The woman who could forgive her abuser. Who could face certain death? Who could make a wicked man like me want to change?

Though I know it to be true, I just cannot comprehend it. And I never will. Because I'm not her.

That's the fundamental difference between us. She has something that I don't have. She has something that my wife held so dear. Something outside of her.

My heart aches with the thought. The emptiness that I hold, the fullness that she carries, even to death. *God, why are you this for her? Why not for me?*

The pain in my chest is too much, an ache and a longing that I can't control. There's nothing I can do to stop it. I need to keep holding her. Maybe something within her soul can transfer to mine. I cry out as I grasp her tighter.

"I love you."

Tessa does not pull away. She embraces me, the sound of my sobs mingled with her own. How can I ever figure out what is inside of her if she's gone? How can I give up control if she's not here to help me? How can God expect me to live like her, to live like Jessica, if he's taken both of them from this earth?

Part of me knows I'm still fighting it. Because part of me knows that there are others that will still be here. My brother. Eliza. Kalen. They know what this is. They know how Tessa lives this way. They know the secret.

But I'm selfish. I don't want to learn it from them. I want her, forever. I want Jessica back. I want Montica to have never met me. I want my life to rewind one year and start over.

"I believe in you," Tessa whispers. It sounds like a goodbye.

In fact, I know it is. And I'm expected to accept it. Maybe that's the first step. Maybe I have to accept that I can't control this life. Even if it's half-hearted, a weak effort, I cry out to her. "Goodbye, Tessa. Goodbye."

***

Tessa Anne Perretti died on a Sunday morning. Peaceful I was told although I highly suspect death is never peaceful. The afterlife, maybe. If what she believed is true, then in her case, the afterlife is bliss. I hope it's true. I hope that what she and my wife believed so stubbornly is as true as the pain I feel now. They deserve better than what they got in me.

Kalen was strong. She called at three in the morning to inform me, only an hour after she found her mother lifeless in her bed. She was quick and factual in her retelling of the night's events. She offered no sign of emotion.

But I cried enough for the both of us. That Sunday was miserable, and I never left the confines of my room. I heard Eliza and Roman on the other side of the door, but thankfully, they never bothered me. I wanted to leave. I wanted so badly to once again drown my sorrows in pills and alcohol. But I fought the urge, knowing I had to if I ever wanted to figure out how Jessica, Tessa, Roman, Eliza, and Kalen lived their lives the way they did. If I ever wanted to break past my anger with God, then I had to stay in that room. A large part of me wanted to curse Him again. The smaller, yet steadily growing- in-strength part told me that if I wanted to see Jessica's face again, and if I wanted to hear Tessa's voice just one more time, then I had to let go of the selfishness, the anger, and the pity I had for myself. Like Kalen told me, I had to live for others. I had to let go.

I think the night after Tessa's death was when that happened. Against all odds, I let go, allowing myself the journey to discovering what truths they had buried deep inside of them. What truth led them to putting up with a devil like me. What truth that allowed them to perform the miraculous lives they led, lives that contradicted the very fabric of what I believe is human nature.

I don't know what that truth is. Or what finding it will do to my life. I just don't know. But Tessa believed in me. Jessica once believed in me. And that's enough.

Chapter Thirty
No Fear in Death

"For it is said 'Oh death, where is your sting? Oh hell, where is your victory?' It is said with power. For there is no fear in death when London is ever nearer. I see her before me, ready to embrace me like a mother to her child. May I ne'er remember the toil of the past life, dare I ne'er forget the graces of the next."

~Edward McClage

I don't feel the same disdain for this man's words. Not this time around. In fact, if I don't lie to myself, I must admit that he was probably right most of the time. Edward McClage was some sort of sage. Some hero whose experiences framed a knowledge that bled onto paper. He was a hero to some.

He was to Jessica. Now, Tessa—beautiful, forgiving, self-sacrificing Tessa—will carry his words to the next world.

May I ne'er remember the toil of the past life, dare I ever ne'er forget the graces of the next.

Those are the words on her gravestone. Words she lived by every day. Ironically, Jessica held onto *one night in London*. Those were the words she had inscribed on her stone. How her parents knew that's what she wanted! How God knew that's what I needed. How Edward McClage became this integral part of my life, it's beyond me.

I loosely embrace Kalen as she softly cries. Her resolve is finally gone. I can't find tears. I couldn't bear to watch Jessica being lowered into the ground, but with each inch Tessa's casket is lowered, there's a resolve that grows inside of me. It's as if what Kalen had has been transferred over to me.

I don't have what Jessica or Tessa had. Not yet. But with the help of the people around me, I know I can find it. I can find God. I can find forgiveness. I can find a purpose in my life beyond what I thought was possible.

I look around this small group huddled next to Tessa's final resting place. Many people I don't know, but several that have impacted me more in this last year than art and fame ever could.

Without Ritchie, I'd know no friendship. Without Roman and Eliza, I'd know no family. Without Kalen, I'd know no hope. Without Joseph, I'd know no motivation. Even Bob taught me how not to act. And then there is Montica, her dark skin standing out among the pale Midwestern people. Our eyes make contact and she smiles. And I know what she has done for me.

Without Montica, I would know no forgiveness. We may not ever speak again, but just seeing her smile amidst the somber faces is enough for me.

Behind all the faces are two that appear familiar. She has Tessa's black hair and slender frame. He has her green eyes. Her parents blend in with the rest. I know Kalen sees them, but I doubt there will be any words. They're here. Tears in their eyes, probably facing more demons than even I can imagine. I wonder if they know that Tessa really did forgive them. Knowing her, they do. I can't imagine she's left them with that shame and guilt for the remainder of their lives. That's not how Tessa would do it.

The service continues with several speeches. Ritchie's is heartfelt. My friend, a newly enrolled college student looks more mature, speaks as if he's conquered the world. Even so, he cannot contain the sobs. He finds my arms shortly after he has finished.

Roman and Eliza are a lot more refined. They describe an angel. A woman who, in our fleeting understanding of this life, did not deserve what came to her. A woman who gave more than most people could ever dream of giving. In my opinion, they described her perfectly.

A host of other people from the A.W.A Resource Center shared their memories, along with some other distant family members. And shortly after it all began, the pastor closed the service with prayer, followed by a plea to use what lives we have left to live like her. To follow her example. A plea that would not go unnoticed.

And then it was over. People left, some stayed and huddled in small masses. I found myself walking beside Kalen and Ritchie toward Joseph, who stood not two hundred feet from where Tessa was buried.

He puts a single flower on Jessica's gravestone, then turns toward us. "I come here a lot to visit her."

"I wish I could say that," I respond.

Joseph smiles. He looks back down at the tombstone, then to the fresh mound of dirt next to where Tessa now lies. "I think that is going to change." He turns to Kalen. "Your mother has left a legacy. You should be proud of her."

Kalen's eyes are still wet, but she nods. "I know."

He nods to Ritchie before extending his hand to me. "I'll see you Monday. I'm glad to have you back at the Art Studio."

I shake his hand. "Me too."

Joseph nods to Roman and Eliza as he leaves. My new roommates both engulf Kalen in a hug. "Let's go home," Roman says. He looks between Kalen and I, who now have taken up all of the spare bedrooms in his house, and Ritchie, who has found his way over a few times in the last few days. "Let's get dinner."

Eliza has her small bump embraced with both hands. "As a family," she says.

I want nothing more than to share the rest of my day with these people, but I have one other thing to do before I can join them. I pull the letter out of my suit jacket, Jessica's last unopened words. "I've got to do something first."

Eliza reaches out and hugs me. "You take your time."

They all know what I'm about to do. I get a nod from Roman, and my family leaves me alone beside Jessica's grave. They are out of sight before I turn and read Edward McClage's words.

'Oh to see the face of God! I feel Him within this place. I hear Him. I see His work within this great city. One night in London is all I need.'

***

I can think of no better place to open up Jessica's letter. I told Tessa I wanted to die here. I learned that she was actually dying here. The *me* that was killing himself truly did die here. Now, when I should be so far gone, so angry at the losses that have occurred in my life, I want nothing more than to live. There is no place more fitting than our swings. These two black pieces of rubber in the midst of all of this germ-ridden collection of jungle gyms and slides that sit neatly beside the zoo of Columbian Park.

So many deep conversations here, all of them seemingly useless at the time, but so important now. I will always love these swings. They must be a part of this moment.

I take the letter. There's no sign to who this belongs. I never asked Jessica who she was writing to all of those years. I never really cared. That is, until she died.

And then, I cared so much that I couldn't open it. As if knowing would finally make her death absolutely resolute.

But I'm not afraid now, because somewhere deep inside of me I know who this letter was meant for. They shared a love for McClage, they shared a love for people, they shared a love for God. At times, I saw both of them in the same person. I fell in love with both of them because they loved me. Not in the same way, but love nonetheless.

I know this letter was to Tessa. I just feel it. It has to be her.

I've let go of this mess of a life thanks to Tessa. Because of her, I know I can't live this way. Because of her, I know I've got to live for something else. Now, maybe Jessica's words, words that were meant for the woman who saved me, can help me start that journey.

I take a deep breath, then run my finger across the spine, separating the envelope. The paper inside is shockingly white compared to its faded holder. I feel anxious as I unfold it. Another deep breath, before forcing my eyes to what Jessica wrote.

Just seeing her handwriting brings tears to my eyes because I know the mystery is gone. But no amount of tears can stop the relief I feel. This is it.

I start reading.

Dearest Friend,

I was elated when I found out you'd be coming all this way. And that you'd be staying, nonetheless. I can't wait to actually meet you, in person. We've shared so much that I feel I already know you so deeply, but this will only strengthen the friendship that we've created.

This letter will be short as I'm currently leaving for my parents' house in Cincinnati. I'll be mailing it there. I've got wonderful news to share with them, but short of Wesley, there was only one other person I knew had to know immediately. I'm pregnant. Yes, you heard correctly. I'm pregnant. Can you believe it? After all of these years of struggle, God has blessed us. God has given us a child. I've never seen Wesley so enamored by something other than his art. He's in love with this child already. As am I. It's been hard for our marriage, but everything was worth it. Thank you for your prayers and your constant encouragement!

As I said, this letter will be short. But I just wanted you to know, I've never felt so happy as I do now! I had hoped to tell you this in person, but I couldn't wait. Three weeks was too long. But when you arrive in Lafayette, I cannot wait to share our lives together. I cannot wait to meet your mother, as she seems darling. And I just can't wait for you to be a part of our little one's life.

And now we can share in the happiness. I've watched you grow into a young woman, and I'm so proud of you. And who knows, you said you'd been looking for a job, so maybe there's some babysitting in your future. I did mention I'm pregnant, right?

Hopefully, this will be our last letter. We won't need a paper and pen anymore. Think of that. Have a safe trip! Please be safe, and be patient, be kind, be reasonable with your mother. And remember, though your life is hard, the truth of your life harder, you're still a kid, Kalen. So, feel free to act like one.

With Love,
Jessica Gerhard

I nearly fall off the swing. Kalen. Jessica was mentoring Kalen. The girl who mentored me. If the words were not staring back at me, I wouldn't believe them. I read the letter again to confirm what my mind is telling me is true.

It is true.

All this time, and it was this edgy, smart-mouthed young girl. The girl I had just embraced an hour ago. The girl who is so much stronger than I am.

I smile, because I'm not surprised. It's as if God is using every person to get to me, even though I've cursed Him for the last nine months. I close the letter and neatly place it back into the envelope. They're really gone. My sweet, beautiful, and loving wife. My caring, sacrificing Tessa. But only in this life. I've been shown that there's more than this. God has made a point to show me through these wonderful women.

And I plan to find out how I can see them again. I look to the sky, past the clouds, beyond space, into some unknown world beyond my own. "I'll see you both again."

But though they are not physically a part of this world, they are still here. Because Jessica left her wisdom with Kalen. Tessa left her character. Together, they've left a piece of themselves, a piece that is still a part of my life. A piece that I know will lead me back to them.

And when I give this letter to Kalen, this piece of parchment that is actually hers, I'll know this: They're still helping. Because that's what they do.

The End

About Brody Lane Gregg

Brody Lane Gregg is, first and foremost, a husband and a father. Outside of those blessings, he enjoys the imagination and freedom that writing fiction allows. Over the past ten years, he has been published locally and nationally, and has had the privilege of working with other authors on their projects. Brody and his family currently reside in Lafayette, IN.

Social Media

Twitter: https://twitter.com/brodylanegregg

Facebook: https://www.facebook.com/brodylanegreggauthorsite/

Website: http://www.brodylanegreggauthor.com/

Acknowledgements

A big thank you goes out to all of you who sifted through the first drafts. Uncle Bubba, Coast, Andy B., KK, Sam, Chris, Padre—thanks for your help and honest feedback. Another big thank you to my editor, Rachael Stapleton, who took my retooled draft and polished it into what it is now. Your editing prowess was invaluable.

To my wife…there are no adequate words to describe my appreciation for you putting up with me and my antics. So a simple "I love you" will have to suffice.

To the rest of my family…thank you for your support and your love.

To God…thank You for Your life-saving gift of faith.

If you enjoyed this story, check out these other Solstice Publishing books by Brody Lane Gregg:

Beyond the Skyline

Alex Lane is a hardened criminal. A misfit. A freak. When he is released from a juvenile detention center at the age of eighteen, he doesn't know what he will do with his life. Alex does not want to return to a life of crime, but he is not sure how to change. A criminal is all he has ever been. And thus he begins his journey.

Alex finds himself living with his brother and his family, a family he does not know. He also finds friends who eagerly accept him into their group of misfits. On the outside, everything seems to be going his way, but inside, Alex struggles to leave his criminal life behind. He struggles with change and with the realization that in a life absent of crime, he must give up control. He must learn that there is more to living a normal life than just choosing not to be a criminal again. Much more.

https://bookgoodies.com/a/B00RY8OPKC

www.ingramcontent.com/pod-product-compliance
Lightning Source LLC
Chambersburg PA
CBHW051129020726
47501CB00005B/1423